FOOL ME TWICE

TWO TWISTY MYSTERIES

BENJAMIN STEVENSON

MICHAEL JOSEPH
an imprint of
PENGUIN BOOKS

Greenlight
Either Side of Midnight
Everyone In My Family Has Killed Someone
Everyone On This Train Is A Suspect

FIND US

MICHAEL JOSEPH

UK | USA | Canada | Ireland | Australia
India | New Zealand | South Africa | China

Michael Joseph is part of the Penguin Random House group of companies
whose addresses can be found at global.penguinrandomhouse.com

Penguin
Random House
Australia

First published by Audible in 2021, 2022
This edition published by Michael Joseph in 2024

Cover illustrations by Catherine MacBride/Stocksy and klyaksun/Shutterstock
Cover design by Christa Moffitt, Christabella Designs
© Penguin Random House Australia Pty Ltd
Typeset in 11/17 pt Sabon LT Pro by Midland Typesetters, Australia

Printed and bound in Australia by Griffin Press, an accredited
ISO AS/NZS 14001 Environmental Management Systems printer

 A catalogue record for this
book is available from the
National Library of Australia

ISBN 978 1 76134 334 6

penguin.com.au

We at Penguin Random House Australia acknowledge that Aboriginal and Torres Strait
Islander peoples are the Traditional Custodians and the first storytellers of the lands
on which we live and work. We honour Aboriginal and Torres Strait Islander peoples'
continuous connection to Country, waters, skies and communities. We celebrate
Aboriginal and Torres Strait Islander stories, traditions and living cultures;
and we pay our respects to Elders past and present.

For Sammy

PROLOGUE

Every object has a ghost.

There is a small yellow backpack – half unzipped, mouth yawning to the pavement, contents strewn around it (a banana, an exercise book, a pair of scissors) – abandoned on a suburban footpath.

Ten feet away the rubber stamps of tyres, resisting clamped brakes, mount the kerb and cut across the path. The tracks come to an end at a crippled stop sign.

The street, a tree-lined suburban road dappled in late-afternoon sunlight, is calm. But anyone walking past can feel the ghosts: the prickle on the back of their necks that tells them *something happened here*. The story of a vehicle careening to a halt. Of a child's backpack left in a hurry.

That intuition comes before they take a closer look and see there is dark dry red on the scissor's blade. The ghosts are screaming now; the scene's memory turns violent. And as the passer-by raises their phone to answer the question *what is your emergency?* they see more red. Between the tyre tracks and the blood. Two words, hastily scrawled on the footpath. Written in blood.

FIND US.

DAY ONE

CHAPTER 1

Claudette

Claudette Holloway decides that today she will be Raphael Lopez.

She's found the perfect photo for him, a teenager with one foot propped on a soccer ball, elbow on his thigh. He's sporty, but not in a jock way. That would be too intimidating. Soccer is the right choice to show he's not a total loser but not one of the cool kids. Raphael's Instagram page, which Claudette has laboured over – she has to spend several months adding posts before she introduces Raph to anyone, in constant fear of the curious scroll – shares football highlights and video gaming memes in equal measure. His sense of humour is juvenile but friendly. He misspells his captions. His deep tan, short curly hair and Spanish name fit his backstory that he's relocated. That's important to Claudette for two reasons. It means it's believable that he's looking for friends online. It also means people don't ask why they've never seen him at school. He's *new here* wherever he goes.

It was a choice between Raphael and Aaron Chamberlain. Aaron's profile picture is a washed-out close-up of Aaron peering into a webcam. He has a black fringe that hangs over one eye. Aaron doesn't play sports; he's a misfit through and through.

His feed has a series of photos of him posing with swords in his bedroom. His captions use alternating caps lock and are rebellious but ambiguous.

WHeN it haPPens YOU'LL all See!

He's for what Claudette calls 'immediate responses'. For the ones who have started making plans, who are looking and ready to spill their guts to anyone. Because really that's why they're doing it: they want to be heard. Aaron doesn't have the subtlety to ease it out of someone who's on the brink. He's there to reel in the like-minded, a short-term solution. Raphael is for the long game. Friendly and loyal, he's there to build trust.

Claudette has TikTok accounts for both Aaron and Raphael, but these exist solely for verisimilitude. In any case, for Instagram, she needs to pluck from at least the twentieth page on Google Images, otherwise she is too easily caught. Aaron's persona is built from a treasure trove of a long-dormant Myspace page. She thinks he's Romanian originally.

She started running out of Raphael's content a while ago so has shied away from selfies for him lately. When she felt a mark was losing interest a few months prior and that Raph's façade was slipping, she had no choice but to put up a photo of a similar-looking Spanish kid in a soccer jersey. She shouldn't have, but she didn't want to burn the profile. The Raphaels take longer to build than the Aarons. Aaron doesn't need friends, but for Raph she has to pick around the school and add a range of the target's mutual friends so he seems popular enough but without committing him to one par-ticular level of the school's hierarchy. She knew it was a risk to post, but she figured he was burned if she did, burned if she didn't. The mark hadn't noticed it was a different kid. They just thought he'd got a tan.

The profiles have to be believable because the biggest challenge is switching the kids over to WhatsApp. Once she picks them up on message boards such as Reddit (for Raph), DeathStream (for Aaron) or 4chan (for both), she needs an incognito form of private messaging. She discovered quickly that if she invited them to Snapchat, or asked for their phone number, they thought she was trying to seduce them.

Claudette doesn't make any of her aliases girls for that very reason. If the profile picture is even close to attractive enough for the boys to want to interact with her, they always assume she's an old man trying to bait them. One thing she's learned: nothing unmasks a fake profile faster than sex. Teens on the internet are very aware of who's trying to seduce them. That's all they worry about.

If they'd known who Claudette Holloway really was, they would have worried about her too.

CHAPTER 2

Him

They'd agreed to use a certain set of rules. No names. Just in case people were listening. He didn't know if the police – or the FBI; did they get involved in things like this? – could actually do that, especially in this house. That's why they picked it. But he wanted to play it safe. She wouldn't use his real name, and he wouldn't use hers. He even let her choose the aliases. She was Celeste, he was Luna. He didn't particularly like the theme she'd chosen, but keeping her happy was important in keeping her out of the way, and he decided that if he gave her this, he didn't have to give her anything else. He'd talked himself into the name, and by now he secretly liked it. He thought of it as space-age, steampunk. Badass. The no-names rule went for the two he'd just handcuffed in the basement as well. They agreed they would call them the Boy and the Girl. That was only partly in case people were listening. The other part was because, if he didn't use their names, it would make it less personal when they got to the end.

Surprisingly, that afternoon had gone as smoothly as he could have wanted. Celeste had nailed her part, which was the only part he'd really been worried about, because it was the only thing he didn't have any control over – as if *he* was going to make a mistake. The Boy – from whom Luna was expecting the most trouble, because, come on, like the Girl was going to put up much of a fight – had reacted the most to the electricity. He had slumped, head lolling with a tiny bit of spit bubbled on his chin, into Luna's arms. The Girl had remained conscious, but she had fallen and was dazed enough to stay where she was. By the time she regained more awareness, confusion (and the weapon in Luna's hand) quelled any rebellion.

So it has all gone fine up to here, Luna thinks, even though, with the injury to his hand, he is now struggling to get the heavy Boy down the stairs. He's got one of the Boy's arms draped over his shoulder and feels his full dead weight bearing down on him as he edges onto each incremental step. That's not to mention the pungent smell, a mix of sweat and deodorant that is what Luna figures fear would smell like. After a few steps the Boy starts to groan in waking, and Luna decides the fastest way down is to give him a quick shove. People tumble down stairs all the time in films, and they're fine. Plus, he just kind of wants to see if it moves anything in him. But this is more dramatic than he's expecting, much more of a fall than a tumble. The Boy lands with a sharp *crack* on the concrete basement floor and lies still. The Girl stifles a scream, but when Luna jabs his weapon towards her, she elects to walk down the stairs herself. He realises she's only obeyed him to check that the Boy is still breathing. She crouches over him and takes his jaw in her palms, presses a cheek to his mouth. She doesn't panic. He must be breathing.

She's clever, Luna thinks. He wonders how old the Girl is. It doesn't matter, she'll be easy to control. As she rolls the Boy's head, Luna can see there is blood in a paste on one temple, matted hair. The Girl is crying softly.

He points at her. 'Put your hands up,' he says.

'Please, please . . .' She's stuttering, and he decides she's not so tough after all.

'Put your hands up,' he says again, nodding towards the opposite wall where a series of interconnected pipes lead to the boiler. He's checked them all, and they are sturdy enough, bolted by brackets along the wall.

'He needs help,' the Girl begs and Luna realises she isn't talking to him. She's looking over his shoulder, up the stairs. He turns. The door is ajar. In a sliver of light a pallid face peers wide-eyed down at them. Celeste. Luna knew she'd be a liability; she *never* listens. They set their rules for a reason. She isn't supposed to be looking.

Celeste sees Luna spot her, and her head darts back behind the doorframe.

The Girl turns her gaze away. Her bottom lip is quivering but she's trying to hold back tears. She raises her wrists without protest and watches as he threads the handcuffs through the pipe and the wall and clicks them on. The cuffs are padded and don't bite into the skin. The Girl isn't uncomfortably positioned, but she is propped against the wall at an angle. She can sit straight if she raises her arms but can't lie down. She'll have to choose which part of her she wants to hurt, her shoulders or her wrists, periodically.

Luna moves across the room to the Boy, who's definitely unconscious. Luna lifts both of the Boy's arms and handcuffs him to another pipe. The Boy's arms are longer than the Girl's and the pipe is lower on this side of the room, so Luna is able to manoeuvre the Boy so he lies on his back with both hands strung up in the air.

After he's finished with the cuffs, Luna yawns. The adrenaline of the grab is wearing off, but he's also underestimated the work. He considers himself fit and strong, but they were larger, heavier than he'd been expecting. Celeste, upstairs, was too slight to be of much use. He wants to sit down.

'Don't let him die,' the Girl says when he's halfway up the stairs. She still hasn't started crying. Her composure is remarkable. Part of him, the part he believes the most, chalks up her obedience to being physically intimidated by him. And why wouldn't she be? But a small tickle in his brain reminds him to keep an eye on her, that her calmness is simply her observing the situation, not making any rash moves, and watching, waiting for her chance. *The Girl could be trouble*, his brain whispers.

Once out of the basement he locks the door and puts the keys in his pocket. That is another rule. He is keeper of the keys: for the handcuffs and the basement door. His accomplice needed to know who was in charge. He's taught her that word – accomplice – which she seemed to like. Celeste isn't the sharpest tool in the shed, he reckons, and she's dumb enough to follow orders, and that's what matters. She was always wanting to be involved in his ideas, constantly seeking his approval, his adoration. They're junkies for it, he thinks, the younger ones. But then he has to teach her things, and sometimes he doesn't know if she is plain stupid or just spaced out. But he knows he can always pull the string of her addiction to his affection. And he needs her. She is an important part of the plan.

In the living room, he draws the curtains across the window that faces out onto the street. If cops could listen, they could watch. He winces as the fabric rubs against his injured hand and he thumbs the wound on his palm as he walks back to the kitchen. He finds he enjoys the sting of pain, because it means that it was real and they'd done it. He feels a grin break out. *We got them.* He relishes the thought. *We got both of them. And it was so damn easy!*

Pressing his cut fuels the memory of when he pushed the Boy. The *crack* on the basement's concrete floor. He probes at the cut. This is a war wound. Hard earned from a battle he's fought and won. This is what true power feels like, he supposes, and he likes it.

Yes, everything is going to plan.

CHAPTER 3

Claudette

Raphael's profile dings. Brad Chiswell has written back.

Claudette hears the notification when she's in the kitchen making a cup of tea. Out of milk again and in a hurry to get back to her computer, she resigns herself to drinking it black. She checks her notes. She has different-coloured exercise books for each target spread across her dining room table. In each book she writes down their interactions: what she's said, what she hasn't. She needs this so she doesn't contradict Raph (like the time she attempted a mutual bond with a target whose father had died from cancer, only for them to reply, *I thought you said your dad died in a car accident*), but also so she knows each conversation's in-jokes, what they like talking about. The green book is Brad's, and she pulls it from the pile.

He is seventeen and attends Alexander Hamilton High School in Los Angeles. That's far from her, but it doesn't matter. She can send someone to him if she has to. She's set up Raph as going to another high school about a mile away. Brad plays field hockey, a perfect underdog sport to bond over with Raph: they both dislike the football players. Claudette the teenage Spanish soccer player has been talking to Brad for a few weeks. She knows that Brad's girlfriend broke up with him a few months back, and he's pretty sore about it because she left him for a linebacker. That's where he's vulnerable.

She opens the chat.

See this, Brad has said, sending a link to a video. *GOAT*.

Claudette opens the link. She's never sure what to expect with Brad, but he's in a light mood today. There are no goats in the video. In fact, there are no animals at all. It is a compilation of college frat boys throwing ping-pong balls into cups from different distances.

Even Claudette thinks it's quite impressive, although she's only half watching. She's got one eye on the screen and the other on the books she's flipping through, trying to figure out what GOAT means. She finds what she's looking for, a print-out with the most common teen phrases in an alphabetical grid. She scans her finger down the page. It's covered in annotations: *no one says this anymore; under fifteen only; vulgar, only if you know them well*. She lands on G. GOAT stands for 'Greatest of All Time'.

She types *That's so lit fam* but decides it looks too artificial. She imagines Jason, her own teenager, sighing. *God, Mum, so not cool*. She thinks what her daughter Holly would say, but even at nine her messaging acronyms need an enigma machine to crack. It's Holly's birthday in two days, and Claudette has a guitar wrapped and ready to go; she can't wait to see her daughter's eyes light up at the thought that she might be the next Taylor Swift. She types *Sickest* instead, but then remembers Brad is a field hockey player, not a skateboarder. She realises she's letting too much time pass: when the target opens up a conversation she knows she can't play hard to get, she has to be enthusiastic and prompt. She settles on her default reply: a fire emoji.

Brad says: *Thought you'd like it. What you up to?*

Claudette: *Math class.*

Brad: *Now? We finished twenty minutes ago.*

Claudette swears aloud, checks the time. He's right, school's finished for the day. Rookie error. She'll have to tidy up soon, think about dinner; Holly and Jason will be on their way home. But not yet. Not while she has Brad talking.

I was kept back. Claudette improvises. She finds the file for Raph's school, the staff pages she printed from their website. She scans for anyone who teaches math; first one she sees will do. Norris. Good enough. *Mr Norris is a dick.*

When you get out, Brad says, buying it, *want to go to the mall?*

Can't, Claudette says, *soccer training.* Rule number one: never meet.

You've always got practice. She can almost hear Brad moaning. *You're either very good or total shit. Too bad, I needed a wingman.*

Depends on the day. What's at the mall?

Chantelle's heading there with Jared. Gonna take a look.

Just a look? Claudette leads. Jared is the renowned girl-pinching linebacker. Three dots show Brad is typing. Then he says, *Might bring my hockey stick.*

Him or her?

Him. First, anyway. Face would be FUBAR haha.

Even Claudette knows what that means. She writes, *Maybe I should skip practice. Sounds like a show.*

Bring popcorn.

Would you do it though? Srsly?

They'd deserve that and more.

Claudette knows that the word 'deserve' is a red flag. She writes *and more . . .* but leaves the sentence open-ended.

I'm not saying I'll show up to school in a trench coat. But that'd make 'em run.

Wouldn't it? Could you get one, if you wanted?

A trench coat?

What's inside it.

Haha, like I'd bring Dad's gun to school.

Your dad has a gun? Could you access it?

Dude. The fuck?

Brad starts sending his messages single sentences at a time. Quickly too. Speech bubbles fill her screen. She knows she's pushed him, doesn't try to justify herself.

Access? Who talks like that? What the hell?

I was fucking kidding.

Who even are you? You just add me out of the blue and now you're telling me to take a gun to school? Wtf. You're a total psycho.

And then her option to reply disappears. Blocked and deleted.

Just like that, Raphael is burned in Los Angeles. But Claudette has got what she came for. She closes WhatsApp and opens a spreadsheet containing a list of names. Next to Brad Chiswell she writes *No threat* and colours his cell green.

She has full autonomy when it comes to picking her targets, trawling forums and message boards for characteristics and red flags that she feels are worth pursuing. She's like a net off the back of a fishing trawler, dragging the internet and seeing what shows up. Every few months, she provides a list of names that are put on a low-level watchlist, one that she, or someone else in a covert building hundreds of miles away, will check in on every now and again. Should anyone on that watchlist deserve closer attention, due to escalation in their language or attitude, or explicit references to a date, time or weapon, they get upgraded, and Raphael or Aaron come in.

She was interested in Brad because, while his Instagram account was relatively mundane, his Reddit profile was a bit more lively, especially after the breakup. First, an Ask Me Anything titled *My high-school sweetheart just dumped me for a jock – what should I do?* Brad or, as he was known on Reddit, *ChiswelledJawline* had replied, *Leak nudes bruh, she has it coming.* Then he'd started posting in alt-right and men's activist Subreddits. Once he'd reposted a video of an Australian television host being shot on live TV, even though that was quickly deleted. Then he'd started lurking on a Subreddit for crime-scene photos. This was not as bad as DeathStream, which has proper (or faked, Claudette could never tell) terrorist execution videos and drug cartel tortures. Brad's interests were more mainstream: Jeffrey Dahmer, BTK. Most people on the Subreddit had listened to a podcast and googled a serial killer and were simply riding the line of morbid curiosity.

It's always difficult to determine the difference between testosterone-fuelled teenage angst and genuine intent. But the reason Claudette marked him was his focus on his ex-girlfriend. That's one thing Claudette looks for in the more popular kids – and what makes her good at her job – the signs that move them up a risk category. Everyone thinks it's just the lone wolves, but it's not. That's why Raph is the perfect bait. Aaron is used for outcasts who blame the world; Raphael is for those who blame just one person. And they are equally dangerous.

Brad had too many red flags to ignore: a new interest in violence, a disrespect of women, a fascination with revenge. Aaron's type shows clear signs – statements of intent, practice on animals, a desire for infamy – but Raph's targets, despite the bland surface, have misogyny underneath. This is why she pushed him on the word 'deserve'.

Raph plays best not as an instigator but as a mirror. Claudette uses him as a mimic. Once Brad had his reflection held up to him (*and more . . .*) his repulsion told Claudette all she needed to know: he didn't like what he saw. It's always a delicate conversation; there's a fine line between prompting a confession and putting the idea in their heads. But she knows Brad will not act on his anger. He will not bring his father's gun to school.

Graham Mullins, her handler at the FBI, gave her the title of 'Oracle'. He thinks her job is to predict the future. He's not far wrong. Technically, though, she doesn't work for the FBI. She's contracted as a civilian consultant, and she no longer has a badge or a service weapon.

Claudette's job is to identify perpetrators who are likely to commit terror attacks. The last couple of years she has been specifically looking at schools, a new strategy. For years the feds have been trying to monitor teens' online activity, faced with ever more shootings – and, perhaps more importantly to the bureaucrats, public criticism about shootings – each year. But social media data is near meaningless when funnelled through a computer, especially with someone like Brad Chiswell. The FBI computers can track keywords but they can't track a vibe, a feeling, that tickle across the back of the neck that Claudette is exceptional at getting. Data mining is fine for tracking those with a radicalised outlook, anyone with a manifesto on their laptop, but it is not as useful for the shooter cited in the press as 'mild-mannered' or 'friendly, polite, mostly kept to himself'. Human intuition is the only weapon they have against those hidden monsters.

In what feels like a past life, as a homicide detective, Claudette hated the fact that they were really just cleaning up afterwards. It didn't matter if they caught the killers or not. Justice is an equally weighted set of scales: once a killer puts a slab of flesh on one side, it's the detective's job to hunt them down and put an equal weight on the other. But she grew tired of the endless balancing. She started to wonder if true justice was, in fact, having both scales empty.

She was laughed at in the office when she petitioned for what her colleagues derided as mere 'Facebook stalking' to be incorporated into their routine, although her superiors let her have a small amount of wriggle room, provided her primary duties weren't neglected. But she knew she was onto something. Regular police work was outdated. Hate used to breed in a field under a burning cross; now it grew through message boards and Facebook protest groups and Skype calls and vlogs. She needed to get inside these people's *lives* if she wanted to stop dealing with the aftermath.

Her superiors had been losing patience with her campaign when an orderly at a hospital told Claudette (or, as she was known to him, Jimmy, a German backpacker) that he had a gun and was planning to use it. She tipped off the feds and they found not only a semiautomatic, but also *three* grenades in his locker. Where he got them, no one knew. He had a date circled on his calendar: 18 March. They'd got him with only four days to spare. The other detectives stopped laughing behind her back after that. But, despite her success, the derision was so fresh that when the FBI first came calling she thought it was a wind-up.

Claudette's anonymity was paramount from the start. Especially when the FBI told her they wanted her to interact directly with terror suspects. She made it a condition of accepting the job that only Mullins and a handful of people would know who she was and what she was doing. Her old precinct threw her a retirement party at forty-five, having no idea she'd been recruited for a new job.

Years on and she's got used to being anonymous, doesn't feel like a cop anymore. She's scrubbed her online presence; she has no social pages of her own. She is anonymous yet has three different names at any one time. Sometimes she feels she's undercover from herself.

When her kids come home she has to switch off Raph or Aaron or Greg or Tim or Jimmy and pretend to be *Mum* again. But sometimes she gets confused which mask is which. When Holly storms to her room or Jason spaces out in front of a video game and won't talk to her, a feeling of being an imposter in the Mum role overtakes her. She *knows* she's doing the best she can on her own. She *knows* every parent has days when they feel like they're just not nailing it.

But she's got another personality to retreat to – several, actually – that feels more real, more human, more free. So when the kids have had their tantrums and gone to bed, she finds herself logging on, checking the Premier League soccer scores, listening to death metal, and introducing herself to new targets. *Hey bud, name's Raph, just moved here.*

She deletes Brad and any Los Angeles kids out of Raph's friends list and changes his location to Wisconsin. Tomorrow she'll start on a boy named Andrew Davis, who Mullins has personally flagged for attending 'rallies of concern', as he delicately phrased it in a phone call. She finds it terrifying, even though she's working with them, how well the FBI can track people if they want to: GPS, surveillance footage, facial recognition. She closes the laptop, rubs her eyes. She's lost track of time; she'd better start dinner. Then she realises the house is silent. No bags thrown in the corridor: plain school blue with snapped straps tied off for Jason, bright yellow for Holly. No thumping up the stairs. No demands for food or attention.

When she'd seen Jason in his new uniform for his first day of high school, she had been overcome with a maternal protective urge. Up to that point, she'd focused her work on high-risk public targets: shopping centres, hospitals and sports games. But in that moment, straightening her son's tie, she became acutely aware of what she was sending him into. She'd asked Mullins if she could switch her focus from radicalised adults to schoolchildren. Under the pressure of rising mass shootings on school grounds, Mullins had agreed.

She knows she can't focus exclusively on the local area, because it would be misusing her position to seek to protect only her children – not to mention that she doesn't want her kids' friends finding out she's spying on them – but she can't resist a glance in her own neighbourhood every now and then. Luckily, it's a very docile area. Her only incident was with a boy named Callum Hark, who thankfully wasn't at Jason and Holly's school, but one a few suburbs away.

He had ordered weapons and restraints online, which he planned to use to torture his science teacher. Claudette had latched on to him when she'd found a video he'd uploaded, in which he was testing out a stun gun on a squirrel. It was truly disgusting: Callum jabbing into a clear plastic box, growing frustrated at the darting animal until finally connecting, the camera shaking with laughter. Callum was tight-lipped about the cameraman, which was a shame, because although the FBI thought they had him on a premeditated threat to harm his teacher, tying in another person would have helped.

The Harks went out with a hotshot lawyer (no doubt houses were mortgaged), who had managed to argue that the weapon was officially categorised as non-lethal, not to mention the fact that they'd never found it, and that without the cameraman's testimony, they couldn't corroborate that Callum had really been *planning* anything at all, and not just kidding around with Raphael online. Callum's lawyer successfully argued Callum's crime down from being a federal charge, which meant they couldn't try him as an adult, and effectively kicked the FBI off the case. Though it wasn't what Mullins wanted, the courts settled on two years in juvie. It was the most they could get, a half-hearted sentence considering the maximum adult sentence for making threats to kill was ten years, and animal cruelty alone could yield five. It was a strange thing to see Callum enter a plea deal for intimidation in juvenile court in order to avoid a more severe animal cruelty sentence, but such is the interpretation of the law when expensive lawyers are involved.

Claudette considers it a victory, though: at least he will be off the streets long enough to hopefully grow out of it, and early enough in his life for him to be educated. That is the best result. She doesn't want to ruin these kids' lives, just stop them ruining it themselves. Although it feels especially good protecting those close to home, she'll admit. Though sometimes she worries she'll bump into Callum's parents out somewhere – a friend's dinner party, a school sports competition. His mother is a realtor and Claudette knows her face from vinyl-postered buses across town, so she'd know if she met her, even if she isn't supposed to – and she'd look her in the eye and see through her mask, and she'd just *know*. It was an irrational fear, but their shared corner of the world was a small one.

The truth was, it didn't matter if she was investigating a threat next door or a thousand miles away, Claudette always pictured Jason and Holly. Digging into any kid's life gave her the same chill that rockets up a parent's spine when they hear 'Breaking news' and 'School' from a television in the corner of a diner. It's always their children, their school that flashes through their mind first. Every target she neutralised, every teenager she crossed off her list was another piece in the larger jigsaw that was keeping her children safe. That was really why she did it.

But right now, her heart feels cold. The sense of not being a present enough mother is creeping in.

She's just realised the sun is setting and her children haven't arrived home from school yet.

CHAPTER 4

Him

She's sitting at the kitchen table picking at her fingernails, when he enters the room. He knows she's waiting for him to yell at her for peeking down the stairs. He chooses not to, although he starts to think about how he can make sure she'll follow his directions from now on. He needs to give her some kind of test.

She says she wants to go home, while looking down at the floor. But it's a sulk, not a demand.

'We talked about this,' he says, putting a hand on her in a way that he thinks might be comforting, but it stings his palm. He fuses that pain with his annoyance and squeezes her shoulder harder than if he were comforting her. 'Not yet. This is just the start.'

She says she's tired, that it's not fun anymore.

'It wasn't supposed to be fun.'

She opens her mouth to object.

'I said it would be *interesting*.' That's a lie. He did tell her it would be fun. Like a holiday. But how dumb was she? 'You can pick the bed. Does that help?'

She wipes her nose with her wrist and asks if they're staying there.

'You know we are. If you want what we agreed on.' He tightens his grip on her shoulder into a vice. 'Someone has to keep an eye on them. If you'd rather call it off . . . They've seen both of us.'

She squirms under his grip. Shakes her head. She says she's hungry, settling on a different complaint.

Jesus Christ, he thinks, she doesn't go beyond basic human functions. *I'm tired. I'm hungry.* He lets go of her shoulder, and she tries not to let him see her rubbing at the bruise. He goes to the bag he left there that morning. There's a box of sugary cereal, a carton of milk and a few packs of two-minute noodles. The bare minimum. There are no bowls in the cupboard and no spoons in the drawers. He finds a mug, shakes cereal into it and adds milk. She wraps both hands around the mug like it's a hot chocolate and sips at it. The sugar seems to cheer her up instantly, like a drug. He goes to put the milk in the fridge, but when he opens it it's room temperature. Damn it. He'd thought about the lights but not the fridge. But the temperature will be cool tonight, he thinks; it will be fine. He places it in the door and closes the fridge.

She asks if he hurt the Boy.

'You weren't supposed to see that.'

She says they weren't supposed to hurt them.

'What did you think was going to happen?'

She's on the verge of tears now, clutching the mug tightly. Part of him just wants to hit her, spin her off the chair and onto the floor, but he knows that if she runs it's all over. He leans to her level, wrapping his arms around her.

'Don't cry. Hey. That's the hard bit done. Okay? We got them. Now all we have to do is wait it out. They deserve to be where they are, and you, *you* deserve the rewards. Like we talked about. But you've just gotta wait with me. That's something that we have to do together.' He speaks to her like the fucking child she is being, his voice low and bass-y, wrapping around her like a blanket. 'We're a team, you and me. A team. Yeah?'

He feels her nod into his shoulder. He looks out the window. It has just gone dark; the streetlights are on. He tries to think things through. He wonders what it's like in the basement at night. He wonders if the Girl is scared of the dark. He wonders how badly hurt the Boy is. If he has woken up.

Most of all, he wonders if their mother has realised something is wrong yet.

CHAPTER 5

Claudette

She tells herself she's not overreacting as she dials. She's tried Jason's mobile, but it's off. Holly doesn't have one (though, Christ, she's been begging!). Claudette doesn't want to call 911. What's the point? They'll ask how long the children have been missing, and when she says since school let out, they'll audibly *tsk* at her parenting and send a yawning officer around to lean against her door with a notepad they won't write in. They might check the cinema and the bowling alley. But she knows what she knows. In a couple of hours, once daylight edges towards the precipice of *overnight*, the cops will take it more seriously. She doesn't blame them; that's the process. But she doesn't have a couple of hours.

She searches her phone for a good contact and finds one. Will Davies picks up. He's driving, she thinks; she can hear the telltale echo of a phone being used in an enclosed space. Concrete walls or the cabin of a car. He also might be in a toilet cubicle; she wouldn't put it past him.

'Will, it's Claudette.'

'Oh, Claude, hey boss.' Even after all this time, he still snaps to attention as if he works under her. Surely he's been promoted past a rookie by now. 'How's retirement?'

'I find myself spending a lot of time online,' Claudette says.

'Living the dream, I'll bet. How you retired so young on a detective's salary still gets me. Tell me your secret! They're all saying it's the lottery. Is that it? You can trust me.'

'I don't gamble.' Claudette is used to shutting down this line of questioning, because she knows how it looks: single parent, nice house, two kids and, as far as anyone knows, no job. And gossip in a police station grows quicker than during one of Holly's sleepovers. Claudette has never managed to shake the damn lottery rumours.

'So you want my help with something. And you're calling me directly because you don't want to call 911. Interesting.' Davies thinks aloud. 'Should I bring a shovel? Who'd you kill?'

'On the money, Will, except I didn't kill anyone. I can't call Emergency yet because I know they won't prioritise it. It's my kids. They're not home.' She hears Davies breathe heavily through his nose as he chooses between a compassionate and a practical response.

'Claude . . .' He draws her name out, softly spoken. She's disappointed he's gone with compassionate. He's trying to talk her down.

'I know. It's only been a few hours. But it's dark. Jason, whatever, he's a teenager. I don't even know half his friends anymore. But Holly's only nine. They walk home together. He knows how important that is.' Then she figures she may as well tell him the truth, no matter how desperate it sounds. 'And I've got a gut feeling, as a mother and a detective.'

'Ex-detective,' Davies says.

'Ex-mother, if you don't help me.'

'Jeez, take it easy. I'm sorry . . . uh . . . I was just trying to . . .' He clears his throat. 'I never doubted your gut back then, and I don't doubt you now. Anything you need, you've got it. Also, wait a second . . . Your daughter's name is Holly Holloway?'

'We thought she was going to be a boy and got stuck for a name. Sounded stupid at first, but we ended up loving it. It's classic. Like a movie star. Marilyn Monroe, you know. She loves it too – likes to say she's halfway to Hollywood already.'

'She wants to be an actress?'

'And sing. And dance. Name me a nine-year-old who doesn't think they're a triple threat.' Her voice catches. She doesn't want to think about things Holly might never get to do. 'Let's think logically about this. I'm going to trace their usual walk home, see if anything pops up. Have you been on shift all day?'

'Just about to knock off. I've been on the radar, though, clocking cars, so not much to report.' He sounds a bit annoyed to have been assigned such a lowly duty. She's always thought Davies was pretty smart and finds it strange he hasn't been promoted past the speed gun. From his grumbling, it seems like he thinks so too.

'Has there been any chatter on the radio? Is *anything* out of the ordinary happening in our town right now?'

'Not that I've heard. Hang on, I'll just put the call out. Maybe someone's seen something.' There's a crackle of a police radio in the background. The audio is muffled as the phone is pressed to Davies's shirt. He comes back on. 'You still living in the same place?' He suddenly sounds harried, upset.

'Yes.'

'You said your kids walk to school, so I assume it's the closest one to you?'

'Yes.'

The radio fuzzes again in the background. Davies thanks someone. 'Shouldn't be telling you this.' He's back on the phone, breathing like he's walking. So either he wasn't in a car or he's just stepped out of it. 'Corner of Wallen and Masterton. You might want to get down there.'

CHAPTER 6

Him

He's come to see if the Boy has woken up yet. From the top of the stairs, he already knows the answer: the beam of his torch settles on a dark lump at the bottom. Unmoving. He can tell the Girl is watching him; on the other side of the room her wide eyes are pinpricks of light. He takes a few steps down.

'Is he alive?' the Girl asks from the dark.

Luna turns the torch on her. She is sitting upright, wrists suspended just above her forehead, elbows bent as if in prayer. Her face, like her voice, does not betray any emotion. It's like she is set in stone. Shock, he thinks. He approaches the Boy and nudges him with a foot. The Boy does not stir. Luna shines the light on his face. Pale. There is no blood on the floor under his head. That's good, right? Means he's stopped bleeding. Luna leans down and touches the Boy gently on the cheek. It's clammy, but not stone cold. Another good sign. He stands up, placing a foot on the bottom stair.

'Is he alive?' the Girl asks again.

Luna stops. He's already checked the Boy, who has stopped bleeding and is not deathly cold. That should be good enough. Besides, the hell he's letting her tell him what to do. But he thinks about his *accomplice* and knows that she won't be happy unless he can give her a proper answer to the same question. He comes back and kneels beside the Boy. He stays like that for a minute, thinking. 'How?' he asks eventually. 'I don't know how to be sure.'

It's no more than a mutter, he is not used to asking for help. He's glad he can't see her face in the dark, imagining a smug grin plastered across it. He then imagines knocking it right off.

Calmly she says, 'Feel his neck.'

He does as she says, using two fingers because he thinks he's seen it in a movie once. The Boy's neck is sweaty. Luna feels a soft thrum. He is surprised to feel relief. It quickly fades into annoyance, knowing that the Girl is waiting for him to report back to *her*. She knew the Boy was alive; she just wanted to make him look like a fool! He is still touching the Boy. He thinks about how he could slide his thumb around the other side of his neck and squeeze. The heartbeat continues under his fingertips.

He stands up quickly, to sever the thought before it becomes a desire. 'Yes,' is all he says. He starts back up the stairs.

'We're hungry.' Her voice is clear and firm.

But he's done taking orders. He ignores her and keeps trudging upward.

'First time kidnapping somebody?' she calls up after him, mocking.

CHAPTER 7

Claudette

Worst-case scenarios pepper her like bullets as she drives to the scene, even though it is only a five-minute trip. She thinks about how close to home her children were, but she knows that what-ifs won't help her. She shouldn't call it a scene, she chastises herself. She doesn't know anything yet. As she gets closer, every little thing she sees screams significance – good and bad – making her oscillate between relief and panic. The road isn't closed: that means there are no cordons, which means no dead bodies. Relief. Red and blue lights: that means it's an active scene with officers, so something's happened. Panic. Only one patrol car: means there's no demand for a high police presence; again, no dead bodies. Relief.

She pulls up across the road, gets out and holds a palm against her window to cool it, and then presses her palm against her head. Davies has seen her. He jogs across the road, a kind of wobbly shuffle with both hands in his pockets, then leads her over to the tape. He's grown up since she was last on the job; he was nineteen, eager and scrawny with an academy buzz cut. Now, though, he's developed a little pot belly – years on the streets have involved far less chasing down criminals than his diet must have assumed – and given up on hair altogether. Despite that, his eyes are no less eager. That means he's still young enough to believe in the mythic heroism of police work, and while some would call it a hero complex, she chooses to see it as enthusiasm. He's after a breakthrough case: he'll help her if he thinks it will get him ahead. That's good enough for her.

The police tape is strung between a bent stop sign and an adjacent tree, blocking the footpath. She can't see much of the path in the dark beyond the flashing intermittent red and blue. She can just make out a clump of black, further down. Her mind analyses it instantly: too small to be a child. She examines the things that bring her relief. There is no ambulance. No one's screaming into a radio. Don't kid yourself, she admonishes: they could be on their way.

'What's all this?' she asks Davies.

'We don't know yet,' he says. 'I just got here myself. But I'm not really involved in the scene. The reason I told you to come was this guy'—he points to someone leaning against the patrol car—'said someone called in that they'd found blood on the footpath. I knew it was close to your place.'

She nods, thinking he has a good memory to recall where she lives. When he told her the intersection on the phone she knew exactly where it was. Her kids walk home this way, their school less than a mile away. Ten minutes across a grass field, or quicker if they cut through a retirement community (which they aren't supposed to, but she knows they do). Masterton is renowned for being a dangerous intersection. Neighbourhood Watch groups are part of her online surveillance. Her local outfit continually calls for a set of traffic lights to replace the sign, crying that it is only a matter of time until there is a major accident. They'll be ecstatic someone has finally knocked it over. Claudette thinks darkly that this is definitely a *major accident*.

'Where's the blood?' she asks. She can see one uniform, Davies's pal, and one detective.

Davies shrugs, unsure.

'Can't see squat,' she mutters, walking back across the road. Davies can't decide whether to follow her, so he just stands by the stop sign, confused. She gets in her car, squeals a turn until she's facing the path, and then rolls forward until her wheels touch the kerb. She's now sideways in the middle of the road, hood pointed at the footpath. She flicks her lights on.

The detective has spotted the commotion. He walks over and raps on the window. She buzzes it down. 'This is a crime scene,' he says.

'Thought it might help if you could see it,' she says, forcing him to stumble back as she opens the door. Her headlights, nuzzled up to the kerb, now illuminate the path.

'Who are you?' the detective asks, but he's mainly talking to Davies, who's come over, as if he's responsible for her. 'She can't be here.'

'She might be able to . . .' Davies stops short of saying *identify*, Claudette can tell. Probably because he thinks that implies there is a body.

'Arrest me,' Claudette says, walking away from them.

The detective doesn't follow. She hears Davies trying to explain, using words like *witness* and *retired*. The detective is chastising Davies as well, telling him he isn't supposed to be here either. His goodwill might help her for now, but it won't stick, especially if the investigation becomes more serious, which it could quickly. She assumes the detective wants to see what she'll do and figures she has about two minutes of grace to look, provided she doesn't get too close to anything.

Now it's lit, she can see more of the scene – *don't call it a scene, Claude* – and she tries to take in as much of it as possible. She mentally places herself back in uniform, remembering how she'd analyse a room. Every object has a ghost, she used to tell herself.

She sees the tyre marks, the knocked over stop sign, and imagines a vehicle – not necessarily a van, *don't editorialise, Claude* – stopping in a hurry. She sees the collection of dropped items. A pair of scissors. Definitely Holly's. The blade seems rusted at first, but then she realises it's blood. The ghost of a fight. Brave girl, she thinks. Her Holly is as precocious as they come, always ready with a verbal jab, but now a physical one too: she's stabbed her attacker. Claudette knows there's an alternative, but she tries not to think about it. The blood on the scissors isn't everything; she remembers Davies said *blood on the footpath*. She scans. There are two words written on the pavement. Barely legible in the dimness, written with a dark, blotchy marker: *FIND US*.

She shivers at the message. Is it a final desperate plea from her children, or is it a taunt from their kidnappers? Either option is terrifying. It strikes her as immediately strange that either of them would have had the time to write it in a snatch-and-grab. There's something about the writing too, something not-quite-right that she can't make out in the dimness. It doesn't look like a thick black marker at all . . . She steps closer to take a look but is distracted by the clump of black down the path, close enough to be more visible. Even at this distance, the object is recognisable.

It's Holly's yellow backpack.

The air sucked out of her, she drops to her knees. She knows not to touch the bag, but she wants to hold it, smell it, breathe it in. She's drawing in great ragged breaths when she feels a hand on her shoulder. The detective has decided she's seen enough.

'This is my daughter's bag. My children.' She's pleading, but she doesn't know what for. Let me stay? Please find them? 'These are my children.'

The detective nods grimly as he guides her away from the bag.

*

'Davies says you used to be one of us,' the detective says gently, back at the cruiser. He lights a cigarette, then holds out the pack.

Claudette shakes her head.

'My name's Connell. I'm not going to play the who's-in-charge card because I understand you've got a bit of a legacy, but let's work together here. Okay?'

Claudette nods. She has calmed down. She has decided she likes Connell. He doesn't have to bring her in, but he's old-fashioned, believes in the code of cops helping other cops. Davies is over at the other patrol car. She sees him lean in to say something to his pal but gets the unmistakable charade of *buzz off, I'm busy*, so he paces the police tape instead.

'So that's your girl's bag?' he says, flipping open a notebook.

'Yes,' Claudette says. 'Her name's Holly. She's ten years old. Sorry, nine. It's her birthday in a few days.'

'Not to stir the pot, but I'm sure you'll understand the question – seems a pretty common bag for a young girl, right?'

'Right. But it's hers. I can tell. If we look inside it . . .'

'I believe you. We'll save pulling it apart for back at the station, if that's okay with you?'

She nods. He's trying to make her feel like she's a part of the decision-making, even though he's doing things his way. Fair enough, she thinks. After all, she is only a civilian consultant. And an anonymous one at that. She decides to keep playing nice because Davies, if he's a beat cop getting shrugged off by detectives, can't get her as far inside as Connell seems able to. She wonders if Mullins can insert her into the investigation if she gets edged out. He owes her a favour or two.

'And you have a son, also missing, correct?' Connell continues.

'Jason. He's fifteen. They walk home together every day. After he takes her home, he can go hang out with his friends, but not before. And if he can't walk her home he lets me know and

I pick her up. It's a rule.' Connell writes something down. She knows nothing places her son at the scene. Unless there's something about the blood that no one has told her yet. 'I trust him. He was with her.'

'Did you drop them off in the morning or did they walk?' He's asking if they've been missing for three hours, or ten.

'I drive them,' she says. 'They definitely got to school.' She knows Connell will also do this, but she makes a mental note to talk to some of Jason's and Holly's friends, to see if she can pinpoint the last time they were seen.

'When did you start getting worried?'

'Around five. I was distracted, working late.'

He's writing again, interested. He raises an eyebrow. 'I thought you were retired?'

'I am,' she says quickly. 'Full-time mum and home improvement expert. I was out in the backyard.'

Connell nods but doesn't add to his previous note. He flips the notebook shut. 'Well, you must have been a good detective because you give a good interview. Concise, quick, you know what I'm looking for. I think we've got everything we need. I need to secure this as a crime scene, but Davies gave me your number. I'll call you if we need you.'

'With all due respect, it's been dark for an hour. They're kids. I can help.'

'With all due respect, you are retired. I have officers. Better ones than Will Davies, anyway; he just wants a big case. So if you try and go around me, you're only hurting yourself.'

'I thought we weren't playing the who's-in-charge card?'

'I'm not playing it. I'm just putting it on the table.'

'I want to see the blood,' she says.

Connell shoots a disapproving look at Davies for telling her so much detail.

She decides she doesn't like him anymore. She puts up her hands in surrender. 'Show me that, and I'll go sit in the back seat and let you drive.'

'I think you better take the front seat first.' Connell shoots her a smile without warmth. 'While you move your car.'

'You're a suspect,' Davies says, as he walks – or, officially, escorts – Claudette to her car. 'That's why Connell humoured you. He wanted you softened up for questioning.'

She sighs. 'I wish I was surprised, but it's a waste of his time. Tell him to use some common sense. He didn't even know who was missing until I showed up.' They're at her car now. Connell is on the phone, half-watching.

'Exactly. Let me get in.' Davies hops in the passenger seat, shuts the door. 'You knew they were missing pretty quickly. After a couple of hours. Did you call their friends' parents? The school? The mall?'

She's shocked to realise he's right. Her first call was to the police, and she was going to call around after that, but Davies told her to get down to the corner of Masterton urgently and she put it off. It looks like she reported them missing without checking if they really were. Too early. Too suspicious. All she can think to say in her defence is: 'They're my kids, Will.' It's not much of an answer, but she believes it.

'I know. I believe you. I'm just saying, look at the scene. Notice anything?'

'It's sloppy,' she says.

This is her first observation. The ghosts are telling her it was hurried, rash. There is evidence lying where it fell. They've knocked a sign over. It shows that these aren't professionals. This is its own problem, Claudette knows from the type of people she talks to online. A professional knows what they want, and that their victims lose value if they're dead. It's a transaction, and if she cooperates, her children's safety is implied. Which means she can control it. But an amateur is a loose cannon. They run on adrenaline and instinct, and they are unpredictable. Claudette will have no control.

'Exactly. But not only is it sloppy'—Davies taps the dash with a knuckle—'it's *obvious*. There are tyre tracks, so we can narrow down the vehicle. There's a backpack, so we know who the victim—'

'Victims.'

'Victims are. There's the message, which is almost a bright flashing sign saying *come get me*. It can't have been written in a fight. It's calculated. There's blood: that's DNA too.'

'*Find us*,' she recites. 'Connell thinks that it's staged? My kids are missing and he's chasing conspiracy theories?'

Davies nods.

'You're wasted on radar duty,' she says.

Davies shrugs and sighs the word 'politics' with a resigned you-know-how-it-is expression.

'So what now?'

'Look, I'm just gonna say it. Humour me. Your ex?'

'Christ. He's in New Zealand. We get along. He FaceTimed the kids a few days ago.' She shakes her head. Darren was a bad husband but a good man. She realises she'll have to tell him soon. 'So someone wants to announce it to us. Okay, sure. The kidnapper needs to let someone know, otherwise how do they ask for what they want? The question is, what *do* they want? I don't have anything. Nobody would think they'd get much money out of . . .'

'Be honest with me, the lottery thing . . .'

'Drop the fucking lottery thing, Will.'

'I'm just trying to find a motive. You know the main ones: love or money. It also might not have been them who wrote the note. It could have been your kids, leaving you a note in a hurry. Look, I have to go.' He gestures to another patrol car that's just showed up.

At least they're taking it seriously, she thinks, even if they're looking in the wrong direction.

'Best thing you can do is keep your phone charged, in case they call with a ransom demand. But you know that already.' He opens the door.

'One question,' she says, stopping him. 'You said there was supposed to be blood. Where is it? I saw some on the scissors but not on the ground.'

'Claude, I'm sorry.' He sighs. 'The words are written in it.'

CHAPTER 8

Him

He opens a pack of noodles before he realises he can't cook them, and eats them dry. They're okay with a sprinkle of the salty season-ing packet if he chews them to mush. They didn't bring enough food, he knows, but that's kind of the point.

His accomplice has, after some persuading, gone to sleep in the master bedroom. He's sitting with his back to the wall on the floor beside the bed, torch between his knees, shining at the roof (but keeping the light away from the windows), because he told her he would keep it on. He wonders if he really needs her. But he knows there's only one way to get rid of her now without her blabbing. He shuts his eyes and rests the base of his skull against the wall. He knows he isn't supposed to hurt them. If they have too many bruises he won't pull the whole thing off, which is why he padded the cuffs, but he also remembers the feeling of his hands on the Boy's neck. It was almost as if electricity surged through his forearms. It made him feel strong. Invincible. He knows he could do what he has to, if the situation calls for it, to any of them in this house. The precocious little bitch in the basement would go first, he thinks as he rips another corner off the noodle cake.

For now, the only thing they can do is wait. He decides not to feed the Boy or the Girl just yet. He wants them weak. Then he figures that maybe he should make them strong and healthy, for appearances' sake. A polished car sells better than a dinged-up one. But for now he doesn't want to feed them because he wants them – he thinks *them* but he means *her* – to be grateful. He wants to be worshipped when he finally throws them scraps.

How long they wait depends on how seriously the police take things. He is sure they'll have got the scrawled message by now. It hasn't been that long but he figures they'll swing into action once faced with the prospect of a nine-year-old girl being missing overnight. Sure, they'll *look* for the teenager, he thinks with a chuckle, but they'll *hunt* for the girl. That's why she's so important to the whole thing. She is milk-carton appropriate.

He imagines what they might be doing. They'll probably be waiting for a ransom call. Bugging phone lines just in case. They won't get one. The waiting is key.

He finishes the noodles and throws the packet on the floor, then stands and walks down the stairs. He finds himself in front of the basement door, as if drawn by an irresistible force. He listens but hears nothing. He gets the keys out of his pocket and holds them ready by the lock. Thinks about what it will feel like. He squeezes his hand into a fist and lets the pain from his palm flood through him, reminding himself to wait. He knows it will work better if he waits, but he's beginning to think it would work either way. But whether he truly believes that, or just wants to hurt one of them, he's not quite sure. His hand pulses. He goes upstairs and lies down next to Celeste on the bed, on top of the blankets. His exhaustion envelops him immediately.

He falls asleep still thinking of the two in the basement. He wonders if he needs both of them after all.

CHAPTER 9

Claudette

Claudette can't decide if she wants the phone to ring or not.

A ransom call says a lot before the kidnapper even speaks. The first problem: it means they think she has money. She's doing fine, but her emergency fund is big enough to cover car repairs or broken windows, not ransom demands. She wouldn't need to bring a briefcase to the drop; she could fit her savings in a lunch box. She'd have to sell a kidney to even come up with ten grand. And nobody kidnaps two children for ten thousand bucks – steal a car and save yourself the hassle. So if the phone rings, she knows she's in trouble, because it means they want something she doesn't have.

But if the phone doesn't ring, that means they don't want anything from Claudette. They might not even know who she is. They might have what they want already. They might have no intention of giving her kids back. They could just be . . . gone. She clings to the message as evidence the kidnapping isn't random. But *Find us* could be a taunt or a plea. She doesn't know who wrote it. She doesn't know whose blood is on the scissors.

She decides she wants the kidnappers to have a plan. She wants the phone to ring. The ringtone is her children's heartbeat. It means they are alive.

She left the scene as directed, without complaint. She could have hovered around the sidelines. Respect for her past career coupled with Connell's suspicions of her meant he'd probably not complain too much if she stayed behind the tape and didn't talk, if he wanted to keep her in sight. Maybe he calmed down when Davies gave him the background. Still, she assumes he will search her house soon enough.

No one offered to accompany her home. It's not like the movies where crowds of FBI agents fill the lounge room with a boring house-party vibe, waiting for a call to trace. She knows Connell will call her if he needs her. She figures he is pompous and controlling but he isn't incompetent. He knows two children are missing and night is deepening, every hour crucial. And even if he felt threatened when Claudette encroached on his authority, he isn't going to jeopardise her children's safety just to put her in her place. As much as it pains her, she does have to let him do his job.

But neither is she a shrinking violet, ordered home to cradle a pillow, swill a bottle of wine and dampen the pages of photo albums. Not her.

She opens her laptop. Chooses a name and a face. Brian from Seattle, middle-aged accountant.

She would leave Connell to do his job, and she would do hers.

Her usual forums – DeathStream, Reddit, Discord, pornography comments sections (if she wants to see the genesis of civilisation's eventual downfall) – yield few results. She dreads dipping down into the dark web, firstly because she has always tracked people's public personas; the FBI uses her to find people who are *unexpected* threats. They have their own department for the dark web, where people build bombs and plan attacks, and she doesn't really know what she's doing. The second reason is two words that keep ricocheting through her mind: *sex trafficking*. Could she face what she might find? A treacherous part of her brain reminds her that the phone still hasn't rung.

The best place to start is with Jason's social media. He has a dormant Facebook page, and an Instagram account that exclusively features inanimate objects. It's not a sophisticated aesthetic, Claudette thinks, looking at a picture of a trash can, followed by a McDonald's sign, followed by a motorcycle. Not only are the objects uninteresting, but he hasn't even bothered to get the lighting or the framing right. But then she thinks that if she pointed out his feed was full of rubbish, he'd just roll his eyes and say something like *jeez, Mum, social media* is *garbage, that's the point* and maybe it's artistic after all. Holly doesn't have any accounts of her own yet (though she's been begging to use TikTok recently), but Claudette knows it's only a matter of time. When Holly does get her way, Claudette will have to be given her passwords, but Jason is fifteen and that kind of supervision wouldn't fly with him by this point. Of course, like all data-protective young people, his profiles are set to private. This would be a major roadblock, if he wasn't, in fact, already friends with a Spanish exchange student named Raphael.

Even though she has a suite of aliases, she's always promised herself she won't spy on her children. She only sent a friend request as Raphael because she didn't think Jason would accept, and she'd only not deleted it because she thought it might be useful to take an interest in what he liked doing, to connect with him a bit more. Not to pry. Or at least that's what she tells herself. She's doubly ashamed to see that, when on Jason's profile as Raphael, a little text link pops up that says 'one mutual friend'. Which means she's probably added him a second time under a different alias. She sighs, realising she's not as strong-willed as she thinks she is.

But tonight, who cares? It's paying off. As Raphael, Claudette can scroll through Jason's private feeds. He doesn't post on Facebook, never has, but he RSVPed to a birthday party. His last Instagram post, a photo of a packet of gum, was five days ago. Nothing confirms that he was still at school until the final bell. Nothing useful. She needs to confirm the timeline. At the moment there's an eight-hour gap in the middle of the day from when she dropped them off to when they were grabbed at the corner of Masterton. She knows Connell will be doing the same thing, and he'll get it directly from the school, but she wants the information for herself.

She's scrolling Jason's follower list idly, trying to recognise a name who would be best to try to interact with. Looking at their faces, she realises she doesn't really know Jason's friends anymore. They're old enough to hang out on their own, playing sport or at the mall, and so they don't come around much. Otherwise her son catches up with his friends online, noise-cancelling headset plugged in, microphone to his lips. That counts as socialising these days.

She spies a familiar name: Lucas. He and Jason have been friends since they were little, and she knows they go to the same high school. She doesn't need to pretend to be anyone to talk to Lucas; she has his mother's number.

'Audrey.' A husky woman picks up quickly. Claudette remembers Audrey is a smoker.

'Hi, it's Claudette Holloway.' There's a pause while Audrey doesn't remember her. 'Jason's mother.'

The word *mother* tends to unlock casual acquaintances. Even if she doesn't remember her or Jason, Audrey will assume they've met through their children.

Her voice tilts upward in good cheer. 'Oh, honey, so nice to hear from you. How are you?'

'I'm doing okay, thank you.' She doesn't know if the police have called around yet and doesn't want to spread alarm. 'Look, sorry to call, I was just wondering if I could speak to Lucas?'

There's another pause while Claudette assumes Audrey is trying to figure out if this is the *bullying* phone call.

'I'm happy to pass anything along . . .' Audrey starts defensively. Claudette knows she's already thinking: *whatever this is, it's got nothing to do with my son.*

'Nothing like that,' Claudette says quickly. 'It's just, look, I think Jason may have skipped school today. I'm not even going to mention it to him, I just want to know, for myself, if it's a regular thing. If he's unhappy.'

'I'll ask,' Audrey says, still sounding sceptical. 'Hang on.' There's a muffle as the phone is put down.

While she waits, Claudette scrolls through breaking news online. Nothing yet. It's always a hard choice between alerting the public to keep an eye out and scaring a criminal into a rash decision.

'You there?' Audrey says. 'Lucas says Jason's normally at school. He says he hasn't noticed if he's been skipping classes.'

'He was there all day today?'

There's the sound of a phone being pushed into a shoulder and the echo of a conversation. Then: 'He says he definitely saw him today. Some students have a free final period, but he's not sure of Jason's exact timetable.' She lowers her voice. 'Listen, um, they're not really friends anymore. Lucas says Jason's not exactly one of the more . . . popular kids.' If a wince made a sound, Claudette would have heard it through the phone.

'That sounds quite diplomatic. I'll bet he didn't use those exact words.' Claudette fakes a chuckle to lighten the mood.

'Not exactly,' Audrey admits.

'I appreciate this, and please thank Lucas for me too. We should catch up soon.'

'We should!' It's far too enthusiastic, and they both know they won't.

After she hangs up, Claudette thinks over their conversation. Jason and Lucas had been joined at the hip, but she knows high school changes friendships. She tries to think of the last time Jason's actually had a friend over . . . She can't remember. He's always talking to his friends online, though. Her stomach drops. She of all people knows that you can pretend to be whoever you want online. And what those people might want. She ignores the dread, rationalises it: *even if* Jason was catfished, what does Holly have to do with it?

She's overthinking everything, needs to focus on the positives: Jason was at school until at least the final period. She's filled in most of the timeline. That is, at least, a start.

She rubs her eyes. She doesn't have time to befriend people with her fake profiles and draw an analysis from their conversations. She thinks about what she's looking for. When trying to identify a terror suspect, she's looking for the birth of a *personality*, the cultured growth (like mushrooms in the dark) of hatred, the festering of intent. That's why she looks for comments, videos, violence implied in a share or a like. But that won't work here. With a kidnapping, there are a few clear psychological profiles Claudette can start with. Firstly, the crimes are normally executed in pairs. There's usually a more organised partner, often an abuser, who's running the show with a subservient, often abused, potentially drug-reliant second person obeying them. Secondly, the criminal's intent is more specific. Custody, ransom, trafficking (goddamn it, will the phone just *fucking* ring!): they *want* something that benefits them long-term. She realises that's what sets them apart from terror suspects: kidnappers are better prepared. They have to plan to get away with it.

But her first step is much simpler. They took two children, one of whom is a tall adolescent boy, off the street, in broad daylight.

They'd need a vehicle. A clean one, recently bought or stolen. That's her square one.

She logs on to Craigslist and checks the car section. She filters by comfortable four-seaters, including (but not limited to – she chastises herself a second time for the assumption) vans that have been recently sold. She opens a new tab for Facebook and searches a local Neighbourhood Watch group that shares pictures of stolen vehicles, each victim writing their personalised plea that's either *Stolen from my driveway while my husband was sleeping from his nightshift – people in this town have NO RESPECT* or *If you see this piece of shit, ram them off the road*. She cross-checks the numberplates against the car sales listings in case a car has been stolen. Criminals use car sales websites to scope out vehicles. None match. She wasn't expecting one but is glad to rule it out. Criminals are better off paying cash for a car and switching the plates than they are stealing one, as it attracts attention from the get-go.

Next, she opens a local 'Buy Sell Swap' group and searches for posts on cars. She scans the comment sections on each, seeing who's asking about price and mileage. She'll click on every single profile that's interacted with each post if she has to, but she's scanning for the tells she knows to look for. There is no difference, she figures, between buying a van to fill with nitroglycerine and park it under a bridge and buying one to throw two children in the back. She's just looking for someone who wants it fast.

She clicks through dead ends for about an hour until she finds what she's looking for on a listing, guesswork be damned, for a bright blue van.

Dev Khatri, one week ago, has commented: *Still available? Can pick up ASAP, will pay cash. Trustworthy.*

He ticks all the boxes: he needs the van fast, he's paying untraceable cash, and he's said outright that he's trustworthy. She knows the last statement is the biggest red flag. From her occasional experience of Tinder, people who outright state something that should be implied in their bios mean the opposite. 'Don't worry, not married' on Tinder is the same as 'Will pay cash, trustworthy'.

There's a knock on the door. She rushes towards it, just in case Jason and Holly have miraculously stumbled home. Instead she's greeted by Will Davies and a female officer she doesn't know, who stays quiet.

'Hi, Claude. You know how this goes. Do you mind if we search the house?' Davies gives her an embarrassed smile. 'We could do the whole warrant thing, but Connell thinks you'll agree we want to move quickly.'

'Of course.' She steps aside. Davies shuffles his shoes on the doormat. 'You must be wrecked. I thought you had a day shift?'

'I volunteered,' Davies says. 'Wanted to help out as much as I could.'

As the officers clatter around upstairs, Claudette returns to her computer. She clicks on Dev's Facebook profile. People over thirty are easier to track than teenagers: they still use Facebook. His profile picture is of a thin Asian man in a suit, with short black hair and a triangular chin. It's as plain and corporate as they come. His profile is not set to private, but she sends him a friend request anyway, accompanied by the message: *'Dev! It's been so long, I just wanted to say hi. We met at that conference, remember? I've just moved so, you know, reaching out to old friends to show me around the place. Hard being new to the city! If you want to catch up soon, let me know.'*

On his page, she can't find his location. She goes to his photo albums and sees that he's inadvertently geotagged a few photos. They are all within twenty minutes' drive of her house. The suburb where the van was advertised for pick-up is not far either. It's a tight circle of activity.

His page is similar to any middle-aged man's Facebook page in that his security permissions are out of control. Apps that he's inadvertently given permission to post run riot. A collection of viral game updates, a smattering of brainteaser or IQ test scores, what his favourite Starbucks order says about him (apparently it's that he's 'spontaneous'), links to petitions he's signed and fundraising pages he's donated to. She sees very little of the real Dev behind the deluge. She switches to Twitter (she refuses to call it X) and scrolls through the options. She finds a Dev Khatri who doesn't have a profile picture but is sharing the same type of petitions.

She can feel blood pulsing in her neck, the scent of discovery in her nose. Davies and his partner have finished searching, and she waves them goodbye absent-mindedly, hunched over her screen. Three hours ago Dev posted a photo of the blue van, the orange-hued skyline showing that the sun was setting when the photo was taken, saying that it's for sale. He's selling it for a thousand dollars less than it was advertised for on Facebook. It looks different somehow. She clicks back over to the Facebook pictures on the original posting. There's now a dent in the front bumper. It's not huge, but it looks about the right amount of damage someone would get knocking over a stop sign.

Facebook personality assessments be damned: his double-shot Starbucks latte doesn't mean he's *spontaneous*, thanks very much. Spontaneity is for cappuccino drinkers. Kidnappers drink lattes. Everybody knows that.

It all seems too convenient. But it works. He lives close, he bought a new vehicle, it's damaged, and he's trying to flip it quickly at a loss. She wonders if she's willing to believe it just because it means her children are probably close by, and decides that while that might be true, she believes it anyway.

She considers her next step. She wants to go straight to Dev's place and kick down his door (physical strength allowing), but she doesn't know where he lives and, as a civilian consultant, she doesn't have access to police databases. Mullins would give it to her, she reckons, so she grabs her phone. Jesus, is that the time? Mullins won't take a call from her now.

But someone will. She doesn't want to, but she knows it's only fair. He picks up quickly. It is only dinnertime in New Zealand, after all.

'Everything all right?' Darren says immediately, without formalities.

'Why would you ask that?' she fires back.

'Whoa, that's some tone. Maybe because it's past midnight for you. And maybe because I thought we were past the late-night drunk-dialling phase of our divorce. But if you and a bottle of merlot have something to yell at me, I'm all ears.'

Though they have a cordial relationship (she wouldn't use the word friendship now) she flushes hot at the memory of her old favourite hobby. He still knows how to push her buttons. 'It's been a long night.' She pauses. 'It's the kids.'

'They must be giving you hell to call at this time of night.' He warms. 'Want me to talk to them? Jason's probably, well, you know . . . hormones.'

'They're gone, Darren.'

There is silence at the other end of the phone. 'What do you mean . . . gone?'

'Someone's taken them on their walk home from school. They want me to know about it, I think, to rub it in. There was a note, sort of. There hasn't been a ransom ye—'

'Jesus, Claude.' He says it as a hiss.

'What's that supposed to mean?'

'They're your responsibility.'

'They're *our* responsibility. How fucking dare you.'

'As I recall, you fought me for them. Sole custody.'

'As I recall, you couldn't get away fast enough. You couldn't believe your luck pissing off to New Zealand with your little . . .'

Claudette swallows the word because she wants to be a feminist, but it tickles her tongue. 'So don't play the father watching sadly behind the playground fence, okay? I'll get them back. I rang you because I thought you should know.'

'I'll get on a plane. I can be there in three days.'

'Don't bother. You won't be any help searching if you don't even remember what they look like.' She hangs up. He calls her straight back but she lets it ring. She checks to see if Dev has messaged her back, but nothing yet.

She closes her eyes, just to think. Her eyelids are hot. When she opens them again the sun is blazing through the windows.

The phone still hasn't rung.

DAY TWO

CHAPTER 10

Him

A banging echoes through the walls of the house like the engine of a ship, deep in a steel hull, waking up. It pulls Luna from his sleep. The sun is high and bright: mid-morning. His injured hand is stiff; he can't fully open or close it. He stretches his fingers and it's still as if he's holding an invisible football. *What was on those fucking scissors?* he thinks, wondering if glue and glitter and whatever else is on a little girl's scissors could give him an infection.

Celeste is sitting on the end of the bed. She's staring at the wall, listening to the clanging. Under the racket, she tells him she thinks the Boy is awake.

'I figured.'

She turns to face him and he sees her cheeks are puffed out, half-filled wine glasses under her eyes. *Great*, he thinks. Just what I need. She says she wants to see them. She wants him to take her down to the basement.

'Not yet,' he says. 'We talked about this.'

She shakes her head. She tells him they never talked about any of this. 'It will work. You just have to trust me.'

She sniffs. She seems to accept it for a second, but then changes her mind and asks him, if not now, when?

'We've only been here one night.' He tries to soften his voice, but he's getting frustrated with her. He didn't realise she'd be this fussy. 'It won't work if we rush it. The longer we stay here the better it will be. Then everything will be back to normal. Better than normal.'

She looks at him. She's hungry – and she doesn't want dry noodles. She asks him if he has any money. She says it softly, desperately. He can tell that this minor thing, those dry fucking noodles, could be the straw that breaks her back. As with letting her choose their aliases, he knows that he needs to give her a little rope sometimes. If he can rustle up some money for some different food it might keep her sweet for a while longer. He nods, acknowledging her, and she seems happy with that.

She stands up and puts her hands on the wall, to feel the pipes inside vibrating, then whispers that the clanging is too loud, and raps a knuckle on the wall.

'I'll go talk to them.'

She asks what he'll do if the Boy's awake.

'We talked about this,' he lies. 'What I have to.'

CHAPTER 11

Claudette

Dev writes back just before ten. Seems like a mid-morning coffee-and-Facebook break.

Brian, nice to hear from you. I'm not sure we've met, though. I've never been to Seattle.

Claudette writes: *Of course not. We both travelled.* She knows to keep it vague, to lead him into it. She doesn't even know his job yet, so even using 'conference' was a gamble, but she's betting most people who wear a suit in their profile picture attend conferences. She's like a medium dragging a fast-talking net through a gullible audience: I'm looking for someone whose name starts with M, has an M in it, has a family member, is a family member, someone who has a dog, has seen a dog, knows what a dog is, someone who breathes air, ma'am, is that you? I'm sensing we have a connection. *Must have been, I don't know, more than five years ago?* she writes.

She makes another black tea (even though she hates it, milk is becoming less of a priority) and paces with it. His response is too slow. She worries she's blown it. Screw this, she thinks. She's used to talking to teenagers who reply instantly and she's letting it fray her nerves. Normally she wouldn't take the risk, but normally she has the luxury of months in which to massage a target. She hedges her bets on conferences full of middle-aged men and writes: *They had that god-awful band.*

Three dots appear. He's writing back.

APod? 2014?

Ma'am, I'm sensing we have a connection.

She slops her tea as she hurriedly puts it down. She writes: *Yeah!* one-handed (she's licking the other one) so she doesn't leave him hanging and googles APOD. Nothing useful. She adds the word 'convention'. Bingo. American Podiatrists National Conference is the top result. She adds '2014'. That year's event was held in . . . Vegas. There are always cheap direct flights from here. Jackpot. Dev Khatri is a podiatrist.

Hey, she writes, *I'm in the area this week for work, and so I looked you up. Pretty convenient!* She figures by confessing to the serendipity it makes it look less suspicious. *Can we meet up?* Her rule is to never meet, but the only way she's going to get close enough in a short time is in person. She doesn't need to meet him, she just needs to know where he is, then she can either check the van or follow him.

She's already searching his name with clinics in the area. She finds him quickly. His clinic's name is unoriginal: Best Foot Forward Podiatry. It's not far. Then she's rushing about, grabbing what she needs. Gloves. Water bottle. Cap. Sunglasses. She can't find the bloody torch anywhere, and such a small thing almost tips her into a full-fledged breakdown, cupboards and drawers flung open. She knows she doesn't actually care about the torch, it just represents everything else. She doesn't even know why she needs it; it's not like she's planning to follow Dev home in the dark . . . She hesitates, then adds a medium-sized kitchen knife to her bag. Just in case.

I have a busy week, but could do Friday or Saturday? Dev writes back.

Her laptop dings to an empty room. She is already reversing down the driveway.

She calls Davies on the way. He sounds like he's with other people, somewhere busy. At the precinct, she assumes.

'Claude.' He sounds almost relieved. 'I was wondering when you'd call. Did you sleep?'

'Barely. We don't need the small chat.'

'Sure thing. Well, I reckon you should get down here.'

'Is there news?'

'No . . .' He hesitates. 'You just might want to put in some face time. Most mothers would be hounding us, organising search parties, that kind of thing. Most of the time we have to hold them back. Connell's surprised you haven't called. It's a bad look.'

'Well, he hasn't called me either. Which means we haven't got anything to talk about, because I haven't had a ransom demand and he hasn't found anything. Just tell me he's trying.'

'We've got pretty much everyone available working on it. He's getting dogs. He's wary of doing a press release because he's worried scaring them might mean they cut and run.'

Claudette reads between the lines. Cut and run means kill the children and flee.

'Um, also, have you considered a reward?'

'There'll be no reward. Besides, with what money?' She keeps going before he can ask her about the lottery rumour again. 'What about people of interest? How long until you get the results back on the blood?'

'No current suspects. Bloodwork is seventy-two hours. Lab said maybe they can get it down to forty-eight. That was twelve hours ago. So another day and a half, maybe two? But you know matching it can take longer. That's if they're even in the system. I took your kids' toothbrushes.' He pauses, then adds, 'And yours.'

'Just to rule me out, I suppose.'

'That's the official line.'

Claudette doesn't have to be a former detective to read the subtext on that one.

'Some good news, though. We've checked with the schools: neither Jason nor Holly are marked absent from any classes. So that closes our window somewhat.'

It's a relief to confirm her timeline. She chews her lip, decides to offer an olive branch. 'I'll come to the station later today.'

Davies sighs. 'Thing is, Connell wants you here now. Not for anything dramatic, but so you don't, you know, go all vigilante. I'm supposed to tell you to come in right away, or he's sending someone to escort you here.'

'Okay. Thanks for the heads up. Tell him I'll see him later. He can send someone if he wants.'

'It sounds like you're driving. You're not at home, are you?'

'I promise I won't go *all vigilante*. I'm just checking a lead.'

'A lead? Claude, you're not police anymore. Don't go by yourself. Where the hell are you?'

She cuts the call, pulls into the parking lot of Best Foot Forward Podiatry and parks next to a bright blue van.

CHAPTER 12

Him

The Boy's eyes are blazing when Luna opens the door. Light comes in from the hall, shaped into a column by the doorway and casting an illuminating finger over the Boy. Luna sees his matted hair, the dried blood flaking off his forehead like an old painting. The Boy is running the chain of his handcuffs along the pipe, making a metallic rasp, until they clang to a stop at a right-angle junction with a second pipe. The second pipe goes up into the house proper, the noise carrying through the walls. Then he drags them back to where he started and does it again. *Scrape. Clang.* It's as if the basement has a strange heartbeat.

The Boy stops when the light hits him. Winces. The Girl is chained some distance away from the stairs, so is hidden from the column of light but Luna can make out her shape on the far wall, he thinks. There is an acrid, sharp smell that jiggles the back of his throat. The Boy takes stock of Luna and slides the handcuffs back along the pipe, starting up again. *Scrape. Clang.*

'There's too much noise,' Luna says.

Scrape. Clang.

'Stop it.' Luna takes one step down.

Scrape. Clang.

Luna jogs down the rest of the stairs, puts his finger in the Boy's face and yells, 'Shut the fuck up!'

The Boy stops. Luna realises he's too close and stumbles back before the Boy can lash out with his feet. The Boy hasn't moved, and now Luna feels foolish for having backed off.

The boy appraises him. 'Tough guy.'

'You rang, I'm here. What do you want?'

'To know what you want.'

'It doesn't concern you.'

'I feel like'—the Boy rattles the cuffs—'it might.'

'That's a . . . we just need . . . it's a precaution. What's that smell?'

'You chained us up overnight. There's no bathroom.' The Boy shrugs. 'Sorry.'

Luna gags. *Animals*, he thinks. Disgusting.

'I have a headache,' the Boy says matter-of-factly. 'I think I might have fallen down the stairs. I need Tylenol or something.'

'I don't have any.'

'Okay. Stupid of me, you know, to trip on the stairs like that. Don't you think?' The Boy is searching Luna's face, even though Luna knows it's a rhetorical question (that's another word he taught Celeste, but only so she'd stop answering back when he said, 'What are you, an *idiot*?'). 'Hit my head pretty hard. Man, to be honest with you, yesterday is all a bit of a blur. I can't really remember anything. Where I was, how I got here. Faces, names . . .'

Luna is ramping himself up, squeezing his injured hand, incensed at the damage he's caused, when he twigs. The Boy hasn't really forgotten yesterday. He's saying: *I won't tell anybody.*

Luna shakes his head, cutting off the Boy. 'I can't let you go.'

The Boy changes topic. 'She's hungry.'

Luna has already decided to feed them. He throws the Boy a

noodle packet, which lands at his feet. The Boy drags it to him by drawing his legs up. The handcuffs have enough length that he can pinch the packet between his knees and lift it, with some effort, just high enough to pluck with his fingertips.

'Just one for both of you,' Luna says. 'Eat half, toss it over.' He wants them to know he's still the boss. He wants the Girl to drag her food from the dank and stained basement floor. And he wants her to thank him as she shovels it greedily down, mouthful by gritty mouthful.

The Boy gives a flick of his wrist and throws the full, unopened packet to the Girl. Luna hides his annoyance.

'Water,' the Girl croaks from the shadows.

'We need water,' the Boy echoes.

'I'll figure something out,' Luna says. He adds another problem to the list: there's no running water. But he doesn't tell them that.

'Where's your sidekick?'

'I'm in charge.'

'When I get out of these cuffs I am going to fu—'

'Thank you for the food.' The voice from the shadows.

'See,' Luna says, taking the stairs. 'Is it that hard to show a little appreciation?'

'Biiiiiiig tooooough guuuuuy.' The Boy drags out the insult. 'Asking us to grovel. I've been patient while I sized you up, but I only need five minutes to figure out a jerk like you. Be a *man*. You're acting like a fucking child.'

Luna is down the stairs before the Boy has taken his next breath. The Boy's eyes widen as he sees the stun gun emerge from Luna's pocket, clenched in his fist, and he scurries backwards, sliding his backside across the concrete, but he doesn't get far before the pipe stops him. He's shaking his head, pushing against the wall, when Luna drives the stun gun into his ribs. The Boy's mouth drops open in surprise and then seizes straight back up again in a grimace.

He writhes, his wrists biting into the cuffs, which, even padded, would hurt, with each spasm. The Girl screams. Luna pulls the stun gun away, breathing heavily. The Boy is slumped forward. He can't collapse to the ground because his wrists are still cuffed to the pipe, so he just sags against the chain. He groans.

Luna leans in close to his ear. 'Who's the man now? Don't forget that . . . tough guy.' He is halfway up the stairs when he remembers, turns and calls down to them. 'Oh. Do you have any money?' He says it almost flippantly, like asking a pal for some to get a round of drinks.

'What?' says the Boy, dazed.

'Money? Do you have any?'

'I don't know how much you want, but our family isn't . . .' the Girl starts.

Luna shakes his head. 'Just, like, twenty bucks or something.'

They both look up at him, incredulous.

'I have some cash in my pocket. Front left,' the Boy says at last. 'If you bring us water.'

Luna comes back and crouches next to the Boy. He took his phone at the start but nothing else from his pockets. Like the bathrooms, that hadn't really been factored into his plan. The little details didn't matter, he thought. His plan was perfect. *First time kidnapping somebody?* echoed the Girl's words in his mind. Whatever. These are just details. He's not the one chained up. That means it's a good plan. He's the man.

He weighs up the risk of being this close but knows that the Boy is probably still recovering from the stun gun and wouldn't want to risk fighting if it meant not getting water for the Girl. Luna fishes the wallet out of the front left pocket. He tries to only use two fingers because it's soaking wet. He grimaces and refrains from looking up at the Boy because if there's a smug grin on his face, Luna decides he'll kill him right there. *You wanted this because you like it,* Luna thinks, *my hand in your piss-soaked pockets. You're hoping I'll brush against your* . . . He has the wallet out now, flips it open. Thirty-two dollars. Not bad.

'Thank you,' he says. Neither responds.

As he locks the door he hears movement from below. A heartbeat starting up again.

Scrape. Clank.

CHAPTER 13

Claudette

Claudette is aware of the green glow of her car's digital clock, slowly ticking away. It's past midday, which means it's only a couple more hours until they cross the twenty-four-hour mark, which is always an important yardstick in any investigation, but especially a kidnapping.

She's chosen to wait because she wants to see if Dev will go anywhere at lunchtime. If she had two children stashed nearby, she figures she'd duck out and check on them. But every minute that Dev doesn't emerge from the clinic is excruciating. Her anxiety flips between fearing that she's wasting the day and knowing that if she pre-emptively confronts him, she could give up her advantage – that Dev doesn't know she's watching – and with it the chance to learn her children's location. She has a terrifying image of Dev cuffed to a steel interview table, refusing to give them an address. But it's worth the risk. It's not as if everything else grinds to a halt behind her. She has to trust Connell is doing the practical police work.

She tells herself she'll give it forty-five minutes, then ups it to sixty, then ninety. It becomes a game where she can't commit to an exact time, because she's convinced she'll miss the opportunity by mere seconds if she does bail out. She tries to keep busy so as not to watch the clock. She has brought her laptop and hotspots it to her phone. She has messages from a few teenagers, which she ignores. No more from Dev (another sign of a psychopath, not using Facebook at work). She trawls forums and comments and videos until the glow of the computer lights a fire in the base of her skull and she can't look anymore. And then she just sits and waits.

Claudette is good at waiting. That's what parenting is, mainly. Waiting rooms, outside principals' offices, in the car outside a cinema. And Claudette waits better than most. She waited years for Darren to drop his buxom blonde New Zealander ('Half your age!' she'd screamed at him when she'd found out. 'She's half your damn age!'). She's done all kinds of waiting for her kids. She's been in the waiting rooms for all the television shows Holly has tried out for: *America's Got Talent*, kids' versions of *The Voice* and *The X Factor*. She's a good singer. Claudette believes this even when she flicks off the autotune of a parent's affectionate ears; they always get to the producer auditions – once even in front of the celebrity judges, though that was cut from the television broadcast – but Claudette knows deep down that Holly will never make it any further. Holly has the talent and the cute factor, but she doesn't have the *story*. Producers really want a sob story; they need enough to make those slow-motion packages with a single tear rolling down the contestant's cheek. Claudette can tell, because they always try to milk it out of Holly. Where is your dad? Why did he leave? What's the worst thing that ever happened to you? Why do you want to win this? Why do you *need* to win this? Holly doesn't realise it yet, but her upbringing hasn't been traumatic enough for commercial television. Claudette has half-joked to her friends that her worst quality is, believe it or not, being a good mum. *When I get you back*, Claudette thinks, *I'm walking right up to those producers and telling them you've got a fucking story now.*

The truth was that Claudette really liked those auditions, because they were always a mother-daughter road trip. They'd normally be put up in a hotel for a night or two, if they'd got far enough in the casting, and they'd order room service on the network's dime, eating in bed and wearing cosy bathrobes, thick white towels wrapped around their heads. She wasn't a hovering stage mother, but those moments with her daughter were precious, and maybe that's why she let her keep applying. She didn't have too many of those moments left; Holly would soon be a tween and then a teenager so quickly. She was glad to have the memories at least, so she had something good to hold on to.

She'd take Jason to football games for the same reason, even though she didn't understand the rules. Jason was harder for her to communicate with than Holly, and sometimes she felt like she could never replicate the natural bond he had with his father. She occasionally wondered if Jason, as he got older, pitied her, if he thought she was a lonely spinster spending her days pacing an empty house. Her kids didn't know what she did for the FBI. They couldn't. If any parent at their school found out she could be watching *their* kids, not only would it blow her cover, but it would be social suicide. Jason once asked her if she wasn't a cop anymore because she'd been shot. She still wasn't sure if she should let him believe that, if that would make her a cool mum.

She could definitely never be accused of favouring Holly over Jason. That was a commitment she made to herself once it became just the three of them. Not only was she slipping different names and skins on and off online, but at home she swapped masks to be a father as well as a mother. So she did her share of waiting for Jason too. It seemed idiotic, but one of her favourite memories was lining up outside a video game store for a midnight release of some alien shoot 'em up. Jason had – and she still couldn't quite believe this – talked her into letting him take half a day off school because they needed to get there early. When they arrived, the line was a hundred people deep. Luckily they had fold-out chairs and a thermos of hot chocolate. By the time midnight rolled around, Jason, who normally only communicated with her in the teenage percussion of grunts and sighs, had treated her to an animated blow-by-blow of each of the last four games in the series. Sure, she didn't understand any of it, and she didn't care that the laser gun could literally vaporise people's heads, but he was inviting her into his world. They were connected.

She knew she would wait now. For her kids. And if she didn't find them today, she would wait again tomorrow. Until the day Holly could unwrap her guitar and Claudette could buy Jason any video game he wanted, she would keep waiting. Because they were coming home.

CHAPTER 14

Him

He wants to wait until dark to go for food. He still isn't sure it's worth the risk, but the Boy's soundtrack continues from the basement, up the pipes and through the house, and Celeste is also getting cabin fever. By mid-afternoon he knows he has no choice but to take her out for a walk. Like a dog. So he takes the thirty-two dollars – that's a rule he's just come up with, that he's in charge of the money – and they walk the half-mile to the supermarket.

In the car park, looking at the bright white – *exposing* – lights of the supermarket, he realises he's made a mistake. Daylight is enough of a risk; the stark white phosphorescence of the store, talking and interacting with people, a whole other ball game. He can't bring her in there. But neither can he leave her out there to wait; after thirty seconds she'll just follow him in anyway. Or worse, she might just wander off. At the same time, he knows that having brought her this far, she'll call it quits on the whole thing if he makes them turn around, and then he'll have to sort her out as well. He really doesn't want to do that, he swears, but he is having to tell himself that more and more often.

'We're going in, getting what we need, and then getting straight out. Nothing else. Understand?' he says.

She nods, taking a step towards the shop, eyes glazed, like a moth drawn to it.

He grabs her shoulder. 'Stay close to me. Don't talk to *anyone*. What do we say to anyone that talks to us?'

They're going to tell them to mind their own business, she mumbles.

The automatic doors slide open. He holds his breath as they step in, waits for the explosion of noise, patrol cars screeching into the parking lot, crackling orders through a megaphone, and then the whole front window of the shop cascading under a hail of bullets.

None of that happens. No one notices them at all. Of course they don't. Why would they? It's just a supermarket. Be normal, he thinks. No, don't *be* normal. You *are* normal. Celeste is already ahead of him. He hurries to catch up, yanking on her arm to slow her down. She shoots him a glare but then obliges, rubbing at her arm.

They work the aisles methodically, like dads on Christmas Eve who know what they want and where it is and aren't spending a single extra second in the store. A twelve-pack of water bottles. A few boxes of biscuits. A bar of chocolate. A bag of chips. He is careful to get enough supplies, but not so much that it looks like they are stockpiling.

Celeste chooses a box of the sugariest, chocolatiest cereal she can find. She says they owe the Girl and the Boy a treat. She looks so earnest, like she really believes that chocolate cereal will make up for pissing your pants while chained up in a basement, that he lets her take it.

They're walking to the check-out through the laundry aisle when he feels a pang of sympathy, seeing the mops and buckets. It's only fair, he figures, to give them a bathroom. He bends down to check the price, deducts it mentally from his thirty-two dollars, decides it's okay, and picks up a bucket.

When he stands up, Celeste is gone.

CHAPTER 15

Claudette

Claudette reaches the end of her patience at half-past two. Betting her children's safety on whether or not Dev Khatri packs his own lunch is too much of a risk. Davies has been ringing her non-stop. Connell even tried once, his office flashing up as a private number that she answered in case it was a ransom demand, but she hung up once he introduced himself. But it's not just impatience that forces her decision: in the short time she's been in the car, she's started to feel uneasy about Dev. Does he fit a criminal profile? His profession is legitimate, his messages are cordial. Who kidnaps two children and then goes to work? She can see from her seat the damage to his van's front bumper, which is the only thing keeping her hopes alive, but it looks less convincing every time she glances over. She needs a better look. And that seals it. She gets out of the car.

Before she shuts the door, she leans over and grabs her purse from the passenger seat, slinging it over her shoulder. Her kitchen knife is inside it, which makes her feel a little better. She wishes she still had a service weapon. The pitfalls of being a civilian consultant.

She walks to the front of the van. She has a flutter of optimism as she sees the dent up close. It's a large concave dimple approximately the size of a street sign's pole. The rest of the hood is undamaged, indicating a minor accident. She walks around the car. Apart from the usual scratches and bumps, there is nothing significant. She checks the edges of the doors, where hands would touch during opening and closing, just in case there are spots of blood. Nothing. It's a panel van, so she also checks the step beside the large sliding door, in case blood has pooled on the floor inside and dripped out. She checks the base of doors, for the same reason. It all looks clean.

Next she peers into the driver's side window. If Dev has really owned the van for only a week, he's wasted no time breaking it in. Several soda cans lie in the passenger footwell. Cigarette butts have been stubbed out in a polystyrene cup lodged in the cup holder. He has three phone chargers snaking from the cigarette lighter and unopened mail scattered on the passenger seat. Claudette presses her forehead against the window for a better look past the head-rests – the van is a single-cab – to see into the space in the back. When she sees what's inside it, her heart sinks.

'Hey!' A voice cuts through the air. 'Get the hell away from my car!'

CHAPTER 16

Him

He races through each aisle, no longer caring if he draws attention to himself. He's already made up his mind that this is it, that it's over, that they never should have come here at all. It's not his fault. His plan was perfect. *Damn it, Celeste, all you had to do was sit still and do what you're told for one fucking minute.* He's breathing heavily through his mouth, the exhaustion of the last few days catching up to him, each breath ragged with both panic and anger. The kaleidoscope of supermarket shelves starts to make him feel anxious as they pass in a blur. He almost calls out her name, her *real* name, but holds his tongue.

He can still go, he decides. He can leave her here, and leave the Boy and the Girl in the basement, and she can take the blame (she deserves the blame, he reasons, after this) and he will just go. He doesn't know where. He doesn't know how. It doesn't matter. Anywhere.

He's on the way to the exit but still casting his eye down each aisle, still carrying the bottles of water and the bucket, which he's filled with most of the food. Not that he needs it. He's also got the handcuff keys in his pocket, but he's not going back to the house.

The Boy and the Girl will starve to death if no one finds them. That will be Celeste's fault as well.

He spots her in the confectionery aisle. An elderly lady dressed in the shop's bright uniform is next to her. He weighs the woman up. She has silver hair and bright lipstick. He jogs up, trying not to show how relieved he is. The woman's name tag says Dee.

'Do you want me to call—'

Luna cuts Dee off before she says the dreaded word: *security*. 'There you are!' He plasters on a smile with as much warmth as he can muster. 'I'm so sorry.' He puts an arm around Celeste and squeezes tight enough to warn her, pulling her in the direction of the check-out.

'You sure you ain't got anything else in your pockets, ma'am?' Dee asks, but the way she says *ma'am* is clearly intended to be some kind of insult.

Celeste shakes her head and turns her pockets out.

Luna realises Dee is holding a small packet of candy. It's definitely not one he got from the shelves. Another *treat* for their guests, back at the house, smuggled into Celeste's pockets. She'll have to be punished.

'We don't need any help, okay, lady?' Luna says through gritted teeth.

Celeste, quiet until now, pipes up to tell the lady to mind her own *fucking* business.

Dee jumps back, startled. He realises that now she'll remember them making a scene, but he's too proud of Celeste to care. The look on Dee's face! He pulls Celeste away and practically drags her to the front of the store. He uses the self-serve check-out so he doesn't have to talk to anyone else. They leave with nine dollars.

Halfway back to the house, Celeste whispers that she's sorry. She's hugging the giant box of cereal to her chest so tightly it's crumpled in the middle.

He doesn't reply. He's flexing his injured hand. Working up the red haze. She says she loves him.

'I love you too,' he replies, but he's not looking at her when he says it.

CHAPTER 17

Claudette

Claudette pulls back from the van's window to see Dev Khatri striding furiously across the car park, his tie flapping in the wind. Claudette straightens and – she's far too old to flutter her eyelids – summons a warm smile.

'Oh, hi,' she says, trying to convey mild surprise as in *Oh, there you are* and not *Oh, shit*. She figures it's best to grab the situation by the horns, so she steps towards him as he approaches and extends a hand. 'You must be Dev?'

Dev blinks. Politeness is the last thing he's expecting.

Claudette rambles on before he can think too much about it. 'I'm so sorry. We have a mutual friend. Brian, from Seattle? He said you were selling a van. It happens that I'm looking, and I'm pretty desperate, so I thought I'd come and take a look.' She gushes out the details. Her strategy is the same as online: confess to the strangeness of everything and chalk it up to the absurdity of life. That way the story becomes nothing more than an anecdote, one where the details – the fact that Brian is supposedly in the area, the fact that Brian hasn't mentioned the van, the fact that Brian *doesn't exist* – don't matter, and when he does tell his partner or friends later that evening, he'll start with, 'You'll never believe what happened to me today.'

'How do you know where I work?' He doesn't believe her.

'Brian told me. Sorry, I should have called ahead, and I came in to say hello just before, but your receptionist said you were busy. I recognised the van and I thought, well, I'd come all this way already. I was just having a look.' She shakes her head with what she hopes is bashful guilt. 'Plus, you know, those car sales websites and all that. I wanted to save time, and if we do this directly, save you the commission.'

She almost sees a switch flip behind his eyes. She has him. Now he feels *she* is doing *him* a favour.

'Well, um, I appreciate that,' he stutters. 'It would be good to cut out the middleman. I'm sorry for coming over all gung-ho, it's just that . . . well, you looked like . . .'

She raises a hand to her mouth. 'A car thief?' She laughs. 'Me? Imagine that.'

'Obviously,' he agrees. 'Let me open it up for you.' He takes the keys from his pocket and slides the side door open. Claudette sees in full what made her heart sink before.

The van is packed full of boxes. Her intuition tells her that a man with empty Coke cans and unopened mail in the cab is not the type of man to repack a van full of storage daily, let alone in the middle of a kidnapping. It's a guess, but it's based on years of experience: this van has not been used in an abduction.

She figures she should make sure. 'There's some damage on the front?'

'Yeah, look, I'll be honest with you. I only bought this a week ago. It needs new tyres and a wheel alignment. I got into a small accident because it drifts. It's not dangerous or anything, I just wasn't paying attention.' He guides her around to the front of the car and points at the crinkled bumper. 'It's cosmetic. Honestly,

I can't be bothered getting it into the shop, and there's a few other things wrong with it I didn't know before I bought it, so I'd rather just flip it and spend the money buying a new one. I'm not trying to rip you off – I'm selling it for a thousand bucks less than I paid for it, which is about what you'll need to put in. I can give it to you for a bit less if we skip the sales commission on the website, too.'

'You'd make a crappy used car salesman,' Claudette says.

Dev cracks a smile.

She bends over to take a look at the damage, pretending she's curious. 'What did you hit?'

'You know that damn stop sign on the corner of Masterton?'

It takes her a moment to realise that no one has hit her, it's just the shock feels so physical. All of the air has been sucked from her lungs. Her mouth is dry. There is something deadly wrong with his answer. 'When?' she stammers.

'Last week.'

It's the stop sign that's the problem.

She remembers the crime scene. The sign leaning at a forty-five-degree angle. In front of it, tyre tracks running up the kerb and onto the footpath. She recalls the Neighbourhood Watch group who have been begging for a set of traffic lights. Because they all knew it was only a matter of time before it was knocked over. And then it was, but not by the kidnappers: by Dev Khatri, driving a new van he didn't quite have the hang of. A week ago.

The crime scene was set up.

The kidnapper chose a perfect spot, one where it looked like something had happened, but it's all been constructed to distract attention from what really went down. And where. That's why the message, written in blood, seemed so dramatic. Claudette chastised herself for thinking of the footpath as a crime scene but it was literally a scene constructed for her. Jason and Holly never made it to the corner of Masterton.

Claudette can see it. The kidnapper would have stashed the children, and then taken their belongings. They would have brought the backpack there and strewn Holly's things around. They probably cut their own hand to write the message. She had wondered how there'd been time to scrawl a message in blood during an abduction. Connell suspected her because he thought it was too perfect – and it was. Davies said so himself: *there's almost a bright flashing sign saying come get me.* He'd be delighted. This was turning into the kind of wild case that could make his career.

As the shock fades, she realises that this is actually amazing news. The search window, both in timing and distance, has narrowed even further. The area has now dropped to the school, the football field, the retirement home her children cut through, and less than half a mile of footpath.

There is so much to do. She has to update Connell and Davies. She'll go straight to the precinct. But when she turns to tell Dev she has to leave, she notices he is staring at her intently.

'There's a knife in your bag,' he says bluntly.

As she kneeled down to check the bumper, her purse had fallen open, exposing her hastily packed emergency weapon.

'Oh, this?' She tries to laugh it off, snapping the purse shut. 'Just a . . . friend's.'

'What did you say your name was?' He's nervous now. He's stopped believing her.

She stands up and he takes a half step back. 'Look, we don't need to do this now,' he says. 'I'll set up a time with Brian for the weekend. You can come along with him and we can work something out.'

'Yes, of course.' She nods. 'That will work fine.'

After he's walked away, Dev then stands at the front window of his office until she gets in her car and leaves the lot. She figures he'll write down her registration. Maybe message Brian from Seattle with questions. But by the time he does, Brian will already be deleted. A ghost of the internet.

CHAPTER 18

Him

He is drunk. He swaggers down the basement stairs with a half-full bottle of red wine in one hand, a torch and the bucket in the other. He is struggling to keep the torch straight and the light bounces off the walls.

'I bring gifts!' he announces, setting the bucket on the lowest step. He parks himself down next to it, rummages through the bucket and produces the box of chocolate cereal. 'Food!' he yells. Then he pulls out two bottles of water. 'Water! Toiletries!' He kicks the bucket off the step and it rolls towards the Boy, who stops it with his foot. Luna swigs from the wine bottle and wipes his mouth with his forearm. He found a stack of bottles, dust covered, in a box in one of the cupboards. He hasn't eaten much in the last twenty-four hours, and he's drunk the wine quickly so it's gone straight to his head. 'Don't say I never do anything for you.' He burps, holds out the bottle at arm's length and inspects it. 'This is shit.'

He keeps the cereal and water with him, and taps the base of the wine bottle on the stairs, taking a slug every now and then. Eventually he says, 'Well?' He puts both hands up in exasperation. 'Well?!'

'Well what?' the Boy says.

'Thank you?' Luna rolls his eyes.

'For?' the Boy pushes.

Luna glares at him and fires the beam of the torch into his eyes, watching his pupils dilate. 'If you don't want the bathroom,' he sneers, 'I'll take it away.'

'Thank you,' the Boy mumbles.

'He's learning!' Luna shouts in victory.

He sets a bottle of water on the floor and rolls it to the Girl. She stops it with her knee and thanks him. He does the same to the Boy, who mumbles his indignant thanks again. Luna thought they might wrench them open and guzzle them down immediately, but they are too shy, too humiliated, to do so. He stands, wobbles and steadies himself on the banister, then shakes the cereal. 'Now, food,' he offers. 'This is going to take a bit more'—he caresses the word on his tongue—'*enthusiasm.*'

He turns the beam on the Girl. 'Take off your clothes.'

The Girl doesn't move. Doesn't respond.

'You sick fuck,' the Boy yells.

Luna walks closer. 'If you want food, you have to show that you are thankful. You heard what I said.'

She is silent.

'Don't do anything he says!' The Boy is straining and clanking against his cuffs. The pipe is groaning. 'Hey! Hey! Get the fuck away from her!'

But in his head Luna's drowning out the racket. He can barely hear the Boy's screams of protest. 'Do as I tell you.' He drains the bottle, places it on the floor, then advances on the Girl. Up close, in the pasty white of the torchlight, she gives a small shake of her head. 'Or,' he says, 'I'll do it myself.'

And then his hands are on her, trying to grab at pieces of fabric, but she's writhing and he can't get purchase. She kicks him in the stomach, which just fuels his anger. He grabs her ankles and pins them with one hand. She's weak from not eating, so it's easy. He leans in close.

'I'm not gonna do anything to ya, I just want to look,' he growls.

She spits in his face. He wipes it off with his free hand, eyes blazing, and then reaches for her again.

An ear-piercing scream comes from the foot of the stairs. He whirls around. Celeste is standing there.

She yells at him to leave them alone.

'You're not supposed to be down here,' he says, standing.

She doesn't reply. They glare at each other in silence. Her throat is pulsing as she clenches and unclenches her jaw, he assumes to quell the outburst of tears he knows is coming. He walks up the stairs to her, breathes hot wine breath in her face. He could do it right now, he thinks, in this moment. Then the anger fades, replaced by a weariness, a throbbing at the base of his skull. An urge to both sit down and throw up. He can taste wine between the gaps in his teeth. He relents and picks up the cereal box.

'Fine,' he says, and goes to throw it to the Girl, but he is stopped by a tug.

Celeste is holding the other end of box. She says she should be the one to give it to them, as firmly as she's ever spoken to him. She tugs the box from him and hugs it tight to her chest, protectively.

'Whatever.' He's feeling too sick to argue. He shoulder-checks her as he pushes past to leave.

Celeste walks down the stairs and over to the Girl. The Boy sees what she's holding as she carries it past him.

'She can't eat this shit! She needs actual food. Is this all you brought?' he yells up the stairs, at Luna's back.

Celeste kneels in front of the Girl and places the box at her feet, whispering that she chose it specially for her, that it's a treat.

She is so earnest and painstaking, placing it down like a cat presenting a dead bird, as if it's the daintiest treat in the world. The Girl has no choice but to acknowledge the gesture. 'Thank you. That's so kind. My favourite. Thank you.'

Celeste breaks out in a satisfied grin. The Boy is now silent, incredulously watching the whole scene play out, the Girl having silently communicated the need to shut up.

Celeste's smile does not last long. It is broken by slurred, booming words from the top of the stairs: 'If you like your new friends so much, why don't you spend the night?'

The door slams, plunging them into darkness. The only sound left is the scrape of a key in the lock.

DAY THREE

DAY THREE

CHAPTER 19

Claudette

After Claudette finally checked in at the precinct the previous afternoon, Connell made her wait an hour and a half to see him. When she told him what she'd learned, he sat stone-faced and said, 'All right, we'll look into it. Anything else?'

At home, she trawled the internet aimlessly. Deflated from her search for the van coming up empty, she couldn't latch her attention on to anything well enough to pursue it. The phone still wouldn't ring. She ordered take-out, didn't eat it, and managed a few hours' sleep. She woke before dawn and tried to lie in bed for as long as humanly possible (she knew her physical and mental condition might make the difference to her children's survival), but only lasted until the first rays of daylight.

While she showers, she remembers: it's Holly's tenth birthday today. She takes the wrapped present from behind the plastic tub where she keeps ski jackets, and puts it, card tucked underneath, on Holly's bed.

She rings Darren to give him an update, but his phone is off. He's probably on a plane, halfway across the Pacific by now. She doesn't leave a voicemail.

The local retirement community is called Calm Springs. Claudette figures that if the name doesn't make you retch with what Holly would call its 'lameness', but makes you chuckle instead, then you must be old enough to live there. It's a collection of bungalows ringing a private cul-de-sac that backs onto the school's football field. Out the front is a yellow sedan with a parking ticket fluttering on the wiper. In the communal garden, a lopsided sign on a wooden stake reads: *Attention Schoolchildren. Walking through the premises disturbs the residents. Please do NOT take a shortcut through our home.* The word 'shortcut' is underlined in red, in the way only senior citizens could hope to instill fear. She knows her kids cut through here, because about a year ago a manager got hold of the school mailing list and emailed a collection of, as they put it in red underlined font, 'incriminating' photographs. Claudette and her kids had one of those contagious family laughing fits that end with aching backs and ribs. She even printed it out and pinned it to the fridge, telling Jason and Holly to pay the old folks no mind.

Claudette knocks at the first building, which has peeling acetate letters on the glass door indicating that it's the office. The opening hours are 8 a.m. to 3.30 p.m., and though it's only 7.15, she hopes to stumble upon an early riser.

Now that she suspects her children weren't taken from the location where they'd found Holly's bag and the bloody message, Claudette figures the next step is to fill in the blanks working backwards, to narrow the window even further. The high school and middle school are on the same land, split only by a car park. Claudette knows Jason would have finished school, walked across the car park to collect Holly, crossed the football field, and cut through Calm Springs. That spits them out on Masterton. Houses on that street would have been door-knocked by Connell, and she'll do it herself if he hasn't done it thoroughly. She wants to check this place first before heading to the police station and catching up with

Davies and Connell again. She parks across the street in front of a house for rent, the name of the realtor blocked out by shrubbery so she can only see the first two letters and the last two. 'Such and Such Real Estate' now reads '*Ha*' and then on the other side of the tree, '*te*', so it spells *Hate*. Great omen, she thinks, as she waits for her knock to be answered.

The venetian blinds are cracked apart by two fingertips, then slip back. A set of keys heavier than a prison guard's rattle in the lock, and a weary-looking man opens the door. He's not old enough to live there, but he's not far off it. He's wearing a tartan shirt and brown slacks.

His glasses are on a chain around his neck, and Claudette wonders if that's a uniform requirement to work in a retirement home.

'Morning,' Claudette says. 'I was hoping to ask you a few questions about some schoolchildren that may have gone missing in the area.'

'Are you with those police officers?' the man asks.

Claudette reminds herself to go easy on Connell. He's doing right by her kids: he's canvassed the area thoroughly since last night.

'Anything I can do to help, but I told them everything I know already, which I'm sorry to say isn't a lot.'

'Sometimes saying the same thing twice can lead to different thoughts.' She is careful not to say she is a police officer, but also not to say she isn't. 'Or someone hearing the same thing can interpret it in new ways. If you wouldn't mind.'

'Of course. The boy is, what, fifteen? The girl is younger, curly brown hair?'

'You saw them?'

'Yeah, we don't like—' He swivels his attention. A young woman in green nursing scrubs is standing behind him with her arms folded.

'I can't find the forms,' she says. 'Tony normally handles them, and it's not like he left us a note.'

'Well, they didn't just walk off,' the man snaps. He turns back to Claudette and rolls his eyes as if to say, *You can't get good help these days*, but Claudette's sympathies lie with the nurse, who's probably over-qualified to be searching for forms. 'As I was saying, we don't like schoolkids cutting through here. So I always know which ones walk past. Those kids'—he jabs a finger at her—'I see 'em every day. When you find them, tell them not to walk through here.'

'You're talking to their mother,' Claudette says coolly. 'If they're not dead, I'll be sure to pass that along.'

The man looks ashamed. 'Look, I saw them after school, two days ago. That's all. I don't talk to any of the kids, so that's the whole story. But, yeah, that afternoon, I recognised the ones the other cops showed me photos of. They came through, going in the direction of Masterton.' He looks at his shoes. 'I do hope you find them. If there's nothing else?' He's already shrinking back into the office, desperate to escape the shame. A spider curling back into its corner.

Claudette nods and lets him retreat to safety. She almost hears the whoosh of relief as he pretends to rifle through some paperwork. Claudette walks back towards Masterton. She may as well go to the police station now, be the *usual* mother and see what she can do to help, clamped onto the side of the investigation like a barnacle. Be *normal* and *helpless* and *anguished*. See how that mask fits.

The nurse in green, now walking between the units, spots her leaving, waves and approaches her. 'I heard the children they're looking for are yours?' she says.

Claudette nods.

'I just want to say, for what it's worth, that, yeah, we don't like it when students use this as a shortcut, but I actually don't mind it when yours come through. They're sweethearts. Two days ago I was here too, quarter to four maybe. Thing is . . .' She hesitates. 'Terrance, well, he's not lying, and he told the cops the same thing, but he doesn't have the best memory. Your kids, you know, they were in that letter, so he remembers them. But day to day, he thinks all the kids are the same.' She surprises Claudette by clasping one of her hands between both of hers, the way she might cradle a small, fragile bird. 'I mean it. Sweet kids.'

Claudette's heart sinks. 'Are you saying they didn't come through here?'

The nurse shakes her head. 'Not both of them.'

CHAPTER 20

Him

He wakes late. There's a fire behind his eyes and in the base of his skull. Gingerly, he pulls himself upright. A half-eaten packet of noodles slides off his chest, gorged before he went to sleep, perhaps. His mouth feels claggy. He can taste alcohol in his teeth, which makes him gag when he probes with his tongue. Every time he moves, the room spins, so he sits there for half an hour with his eyes closed. Eventually the need to piss overcomes the nausea. He pushes himself up and pads down the hall.

The house smells worse than the basement, he thinks. He opens the toilet door and instantly retches. The room is full of vomit. Most of it's in the bowl, but there is some spattered on the floor. Even some on the walls. He wraps an elbow across his nose and mouth and leans forward to flush. Nothing happens. No running water, he remembers. He's been pissing in the yard, and they've been saving their one flush for emergencies. Evidently he's been on his knees all night and has run it dry.

He goes back to the bedroom for another lie-down, but he's distracted by the smell. The front of his T-shirt is chalky with dried vomit. They've only brought one change of clothes each, but the hell he's wearing this any longer. He heads to the kitchen, takes off his shirt and uses half of one of the water bottles (that's right, he remembers, they went to the shops to get water!) to wring his shirt in the sink. He tries to drink the other half, but gags after only a few mouthfuls. He pours some into his hand and splashes his forehead, then wipes the back of his neck.

He shuts his eyes and thinks. He has little memory of last night. He remembers finding a stash of wine. After that, not so much.

Eventually, he remembers where Celeste is.

CHAPTER 21

Claudette

The precinct still feels almost alien to Claudette; she's had very little cause to visit after her fake retirement party. Police stations, she's always found, are rarely the hive of activity that films and television shows pretend they are. It actually sounds like a newsroom, a background of clicking and typing under a murmur of quiet conversation. No one's yelling 'I'm gonna get this son of a bitch'. So she's not disconcerted by the quiet. She didn't expect everyone to be at battle stations for her kids. There are other cases. Connell will have a briefing room, sure, but it will be him and maybe another detective, tops, with uniforms to call on if he needs them. It's not the all-hands-on-deck, this-time-it's-personal approach of Hollywood: casework is a boring series of compromises between public safety, staff levels and overtime, and the longer her kids are missing, the more unbalanced that equation will get, until the team is whittled down to one grizzled detective working a cold case. She's lucky to have Davies hanging around to add some extra manpower.

The precinct waiting room has only one other person in it, a woman who looks like she's dressed for work, not for arrest, legs crossed while she reads a document. Not a lawyer. Maybe waiting to bail someone out. Her expression of tight-lipped fury suggests she's been pulled away from something important and is now waiting for someone. Considering her age and the time of day, Claudette figures it might be a juvenile. She guesses drinking, held overnight. She knows this woman's look all too well. She saw it on Callum Hark's parents, Wendy and Anthony, a few months ago, when he'd been arrested for plotting to torture his science teacher. It's not really a look of pain, anger or even disappointment; it's all three, of course, but it's also more. It's a look of discovery. A look that says: *so, this is my son.*

Connell comes out to meet Claudette, shakes her hand and thanks her for coming in again. He looks busy but not harried. He fills her in on where he's got to as he leads her into his office. Same as her, he's tracked the final sighting of Holly and Jason to the retirement home, citing Terrance's witness statement as he sits down.

Claudette tells him he's got it wrong. She remembers the rest of the nurse's haunting statement: *'Two days ago, it was just the girl. On her own. I thought she was in a hurry, but now, after what you and the police are saying, I don't think I knew what I was looking at. She wasn't in a rush. She was scared.'* Claudette repeats it verbatim to Connell.

Connell sweeps some papers off a satellite map he has on his desk. He picks up a pen and taps it on the map. Claudette can see what he's thinking: Jason was taken first, Holly ran, and got as far as the retirement community. Their window is getting very small indeed. They have traced it back to the football field or the school car park.

'This is too well planned,' Claudette surmises. 'Someone was waiting for them after school.'

'I'll have to verify what you're telling me, as your interview with the nurse is not official. But, taking it on faith, I agree.' He drops the pen and rubs his brow. He looks exhausted. 'I just . . .' He pauses, deciding whether to let his guard down. 'I've looked for a lot of missing people, and I just don't *get* it. The staging of it all. They scouted that location, the note, the blood, the backpack: it's peacocking. And any other crime, I'd buy it. But kidnap? Either they want a ransom and we would expect them to make themselves known, or they just want the – I'm sorry but it's true – they just want the kids. But then why make themselves known at all?'

'You're wondering why they're setting up a distraction, when they're the ones creating the attention in the first place.'

Connell nods. 'It's a performance. It's almost like their point is to make it look like a regular kidnapping.'

Claudette thinks about this. It does all feel very strange but at the same time very deliberate. She feels like she's getting closer, but she can't quite see all the connections yet. 'What about the blood?' she asks. 'If it's all a set-up, could it be the kidnapper's own? Or pig's blood or something?'

'We haven't got the lab results back yet. I wouldn't want to get your hopes up,' Connell says, but she can tell he's thinking the same thing. He sighs. 'I'm sorry to do this, but do you mind if I ask you some more . . .' He clears his throat. 'Some personal questions?'

'After all this? You still think . . .'

'If they *are* putting on a show,' Connell says calmly, 'we have to figure out who they're putting it on for.' He raps his knuckles absent-mindedly on the desk. 'You know, in college I played baseball. I was good. Like, without tooting my own horn, I was *very* good. I was being scouted by all the major league teams. And then'—he shrugs—'I decided I wanted to be a cop. So I quit. Imagine that, a college kid, not even nineteen, throwing all that away to go to the police academy.'

'I'm not great on sports metaphors,' Claudette says. 'Are you trying to tell me my kids are important to you because you stopped playing baseball?'

'No. I'm trying to tell you I just quit because I wanted to. It was simple. But people don't like it when you turn your back on something they'd give their right arm for. So they said all kinds of things about me. People will believe whatever they want when you don't tell them anything. They thought I was injured but hiding it. They thought I got banned for being a drug cheat. They thought I got a girl pregnant. You see where I'm going with this?'

'You didn't do any of that,' she says. 'You just quit.'

'I just quit.' He lets it sink in. 'By all reports you were a good detective. Better than good. The information you've brought me over the last two days has been useful, and I appreciate it, and I don't often say that to people who think they're *helping*'—he puts the word in air quotes—'an investigation. But you're a subject of speculation around here; you must know that. A star detective abandons a glittering career? Someone told me it was a sex scandal. Someone else said you're undercover so deep none of us are allowed to know. Will Davies told me you won the damn lottery, while others say you took bribes. I don't believe any of them. I'm not asking you to tell me why you quit. All I'm saying is, maybe it's worth thinking about what people think about *you*. If anyone has a grudge, anyone has a reason, be it real or perceived. Davies mentioned you have an ex-husband . . .'

'We have an amicable relationship. He's in New Zealand.'

'We'll check that.' Connell jots a note. 'And, listen, I understand the need to be discreet, but it would factor into my opinion on a ransom motive if you've, say, had a significant windfall recently.'

She almost laughs at his awkward phrasing. 'I didn't win the lottery.' She pauses. 'Aren't you gonna write that down?'

'I think I can remember it. That's enough for now.' He stands. 'It would be okay with me if you wanted to ride along with Davies today. His heart's in the right place but, you know, treat him with kid gloves. There's a reason he hasn't been promoted since you left: he's not great on the big cases.'

'A bit harsh, sir.' Claudette finds she's called him 'sir' accidentally. Not in a subservient way, but as a reflex from standing in the precinct office again. He seems surprised, but pleased. She lets him have it, hoping it endears her to him further.

'You haven't been here in a few years,' he says. 'All I'm saying is he needs a big case, so just make sure his priorities are in the right order. I don't need someone kicking down doors and shooting the wrong people, so just . . .' He thinks of how to phrase it. 'I'm bringing you in on this, but I'm giving you a leash. He'll do as a chaperone and can flash a badge if it helps you get somewhere. Understand?'

She nods.

'We hope to get the blood results back soon. I'll keep you in the loop.'

She turns his words over in her head as she leaves his office. He posed the same questions she's been grappling with since the very first night. Where was the motive? Connell laid it out astutely: *no one* knew who she was or why she'd left. Her association with the FBI was dangerous, but it was secret; she was scrubbed clean, she was sure. No one could have found that out . . . could they?

CHAPTER 22

Him

He is still on shaky legs as he opens the basement door. The only difference from the last time is now there is one more pair of eyes staring up at him.

Celeste is sitting with the Girl. She's got her back against the wall and they are holding hands. A regular girl's night in. The Boy is asleep or passed out, the torn-open cereal box by his feet. Both water bottles are empty. The bucket is on the opposite side of the room, as far away as it can be. Celeste must have helped each of them and then moved it. He shakes his head in disgust. She is not supposed to be their friend. She is not supposed to be covered in their piss and their shit. She is nothing to them. She is *his* and *his* alone.

'Come on,' he says. Like beckoning a dog.

Celeste pulls herself away from the Girl, who gives her a warm smile as if to say, *it's okay, go*, and walks to the stairs with her head down. She doesn't say anything as she moves past him. He reaches out a forearm across Celeste's collarbone. She stops.

'I'm struggling,' he says to the basement, as if they are his audience, 'to see who's in charge here anymore.' He grabs Celeste's wrist and yanks her back down the stairs. 'You're down here cleaning up their shit now, are you?'

Celeste sniffles. She nods, but maybe only because of how hard he is squeezing her wrist. He wrenches her back over to the Girl.

'Leave her alone,' the Girl says.

'Oh, you've made a friend.' He sneers at Celeste. 'You know, it's this kind of . . . behaviour that makes me wonder just whose side you're really on.' He lets go of her wrist. In his other hand he is holding the stun gun. 'So show me'—he holds out the stun gun— 'whose side you're going to choose.'

Celeste gives her head a little shake, all the rebellion she can muster.

'Take it.'

She slowly takes the stun gun. Turns it over in her hand. The Girl is just watching, not saying anything.

'Use it on her,' he says. He sees the horror dawn on Celeste's face. 'Unless you like it down here.'

Celeste nods slowly. He knows she'd want out of here above all else. She's chewing her lip, tears rolling down her cheeks. She falls to her knees next to the Girl. The Girl is not backing away or struggling against her chains like the Boy did. She remains resolute, holds her chin up, and forces out a forgiving smile.

'It's okay,' the Girl says.

Celeste stammers an apology. She turns back towards Luna, appealing, but he's standing with his arms folded, waiting.

'She's not your friend,' he says firmly. It's unclear who he's talking to.

'It's okay,' the Girl whispers again. She shuts her eyes. 'Do what you have to.'

With her eyes, Celeste is still begging for a reprieve, but he won't give it. He nods. *Do it.*

Celeste whispers that she's sorry one last time, reaches in as if for a hug, and buries the stun gun into the Girl's back.

CHAPTER 23

Claudette

Late afternoon, Claudette rides with Davies down Masterton, back towards Calm Springs. She wants to keep shrinking the search window and, now they've ruled out everything after the retirement village, to interview all the staff and the residents herself. She doesn't notice that Davies is uncharacteristically quiet until he pulls up outside Calm Springs. Something looks different but she can't peg it: parking tickets still flutter on the yellow car that doesn't understand 'Visitor's Parking'; the half-hidden real estate sign across the road still reads *Hate*; the sign warning schoolchildren still shares its curmudgeonly message from the flowerbed. She's trying to figure out what's bugging her when she realises Davies hasn't spoken the entire car ride. He kills the engine and turns to her.

'I've got something I need to talk to you about,' he says. His voice is low, awkward and shy, as if he's driving a first date home and asking for a kiss. But there is a seriousness to him that is unfamiliar enough to give her chills. 'This is hard for me to say, Claude, and, listen, I know you'll do anything to get your kids back . . .'

Suddenly, an old conversation crashes into her head.

Be honest with me, the lottery thing . . .

Drop the fucking lottery thing, Will.

He thinks she has money, she realises. A lot of it. He's even told Connell about it. There's been no ransom demand, but he's asked too many questions about her finances. Is he simply waiting to be sure he can get what he wants? Or is he waiting for her to post a reward? He did suggest one, after all. Was he planning to collect it anonymously?

He told her he'd struggled to advance to due to politics. But now Connell's words echo in her memory: *He needs a big case.*

They knew the entire crime scene was so dramatic, so performative. What if it was designed to be a big story? To make him a hero? This case is as sensational as they come; it will go viral. Hell, he probably imagined her handing over his reward check, smiling as she unwittingly paid a hidden ransom, while he wore a medal pinned to his chest in front of the entire country's news. Connell asked who the kidnapper was performing for. But maybe it wasn't her. Maybe it was *everyone.*

She tries to keep her expression neutral. Her mind is rattling off reasons why it can't be true, but he looks so agitated, shifting in his seat – she becomes very aware of his gun, holstered on his right hip – as he tries to find the words. She already decides she'll do whatever he says, unreservedly.

'Someone called the cops,' he says simply.

Claudette has worked herself into such a panic that it takes her a few seconds to process that Davies is not making a threat or a confession. When she does, she is filled with shame: partly for doubting him in the first place and partly for what she knows is coming next.

'Around four, yesterday. You're lucky I was the first respondent. I shouldn't have been, but I had a feeling it had something to do with you, so I said I'd take it, drove across town.'

Claudette swallows. 'I didn't think he'd call the cops.' It's not much of an excuse.

'You had a knife.' He chews his lip. 'I did the interview. Nice enough guy. For what it's worth, he didn't really care if you were casing his van; he was more worried you'd hurt someone or yourself. I took notes. When I got back to my car, I tore them up. Reported back as a false alarm. Too bad you didn't win the lottery, because you owe me.'

'Thank you,' she murmurs, like a kid who's just been let off detention.

'I don't need thanks. I need you to control yourself. Calm down. Trust us. You're one of us – well, you were, you still are, whatever – civilian or not. Everyone here is trying to help you.'

'I'm trying to trust, but it's been nearly forty-eight hours. Connell's keeping me at arm's length. He says you're only helping me because you want a high-profile case. That everyone finds you di—' She stops herself but the damage is done. She regrets it. It's nothing better than petty mud-slinging.

Davies goes quiet. He swallows. 'Connell told you I'm difficult?'

'I'm sorry, I shouldn't have . . .'

'No, it's fair enough for you to think that. I know how it looks. I've been here for years and I'm still the same rank as when I started. Anyone else would be desperate to break a case.' He looks like he might leave it there but then shrugs animatedly. 'There was a bust. Cash and drugs. And then, well, some of it went missing. I was a part of it. And then I didn't want to be a part of it anymore. Some people got busted. And, well, that's what makes a man *difficult*. That's what makes a man unpromotable. No one wants to be a turncoat's partner. No one has my back if things get hairy. And then you called me, and I admit I was selfish in wanting to be involved. I just want to do something good.'

She understands. She's spent the last few days just wanting to feel like she's doing *something*. She needs that momentum, otherwise she fears she'll have to live the rest of her life remembering how she let her children die by sitting at the kitchen table waiting for the phone to ring. 'I trust you,' she says. She thinks back to the first night at the footpath crime scene, Davies being brushed off by the man she thought was his partner. His lament that he'd been on the speed radar all day. Connell's warning to her. *Politics.* Davies is an outcast, and her words sound hollow after what she's accused him of in her mind. There's only one way to really make it clear. She takes a breath. 'I'm not retired. I haven't won the lottery. I'm a consultant for the FBI.'

Time seems to suspend in the car, and then Davies yells, 'You're a spook?!' He lifts his hands off the wheel for a second, but only to smack them down again with excitement. The old Will Davies is back. 'The retirement party was faked? That's some black-ops shit!'

'I'm not actually a cop, or an agent, I'm treated as a civilian. No one, and I mean no one, knows about it. I work on tracking terror suspects, mainly online.'

Davies thinks for a minute. 'If you're deep in one of these organisations . . . I mean, anyone the FBI is interested in is gonna be bad news. They'll have no problem taking kids. Is it possible anyone could have tracked you down?'

'It's not that kind of undercover.'

'Isn't it? Terrorists are pretty well funded, from what I hear. The only thing more resourceful than a terrorist cell'—he flashes her a grin—'is a vengeful mother.'

'I don't know how to say this. I track teenagers, not . . .' Something dawns on her. 'Hang on. What did you just say? About me?'

'Oh, it was a joke. I just meant that I've never seen anyone as determined as you've been these last few days. I wasn't calling you a terrorist or anyth—'

'Shut up for a second.' Her mind is whirling. Everything is crashing into place. It dawns on her. 'I know what's different.'

'Claude, you've lost me.'

'That yellow car. Yesterday it had only one parking ticket. Today it has two.' She points out the window. Only now has she realised it's the fluttering of parking tickets that isn't right. 'Run the plates.'

Davies is already punching the numberplate into the console. But she knows what it will come up with already. Just as she knows that when they probe deeper into the staff roster of Calm Springs, they'll find a man known as Tony, who hasn't shown up to work in a few days. Claudette remembers the nurse snapping at her boss. *Tony normally handles it, and it's not like he left us a note.*

'Got it,' Davies says.

'Hark,' Claudette whispers ahead of him. 'Wendy and Anthony Hark.'

'How'd you know that? Jesus.' He squints at the computer screen, confused. 'I remember now. His name's on the staff list. But aside from that the name doesn't mean anything to me.'

The only thing more resourceful than a terrorist cell is a vengeful mother.

Claudette is rapidly piecing it together. The FBI didn't find the stun gun and handcuffs when they searched Callum Hark's bedroom. Callum's online order and payment on his personal PayPal account, linked to his dad's credit card, was enough to send him to juvie, but the weapons were unaccounted for. What if he hadn't got rid of them at all? A stun gun and two pairs of handcuffs would be more than enough to handle two children.

Who are they performing for? The theatrics are taunts. They don't want a ransom, but it is deeply personal.

'Their boy, Callum. I put him in juvie.' She can barely form the words.

Davies starts the car. He doesn't need to ask her where they're going.

'We've finally got motive.'

He nods. 'You took their boy. They took yours.'

CHAPTER 24

Him

Celeste – he's so fucking sick of that name – hasn't talked to him since he let her out of the basement. At first she sulked in the bedroom, but the smell from the toilet made the top floor near-uninhabitable, so she's joined him downstairs. Her eyes are red-rimmed and she keeps giving him a new look, one he doesn't quite understand but definitely doesn't like. He can't describe it. It's not a change in her eyes or her face, it's in her entire presence. Normally he'd needle her, yell at her, test her obedience, but not this morning. He makes a note to be extra careful not to turn his back on her.

He is sitting in the front room, peeking through the curtains onto the street. It's much quieter than he expected, and while he certainly doesn't want to see police cruisers carving gouges in the front lawn or cops with straight arms, guns out, leaping up the front steps, he is disappointed not to hear a few blaring sirens go past. He has a niggling feeling that today is special. Day Three. There's something about it he just can't put his finger on, but he decides it's a good feeling – excitement that it is almost over.

They're all starving now. He's shaken his sickness and now wants food. McDonald's. KFC. Something deep-fried. He almost marches down to the basement and takes the cereal back, but he doesn't want to see another red-rimmed judgemental look from Celeste if he's busted stealing food from their prisoners. His injured hand now feels like a boulder hanging from his wrist. It's so puffed up he wonders if it's infected. He doesn't have the stomach to unwrap it and look. His plan has been perfect. So what if the cut got infected? That's just details. Day Three, he thinks again. It must be almost over. He peels back the curtains again, hoping for some activity. Are they searching at all? Don't they care?

She calls to him as he walks past the kitchen. She is sitting at the table playing with a mobile phone. Without looking up, she tells him they're in the news.

'How the hell did you get into this?' He snatches the phone from her. It's the Boy's. Luna took it at the very start. 'You, with all your genius, hacked a phone?'

She gives him that new look and tells him the Girl gave her the passcode last night in case she needed to call for help. She's bluffing about calling for help, he realises, but his skin prickles all the same. He realises what her new look is: *courage*. It's terrifying.

He looks at the phone. 'Have you read it?'

She admits she's only read a little bit, asks if he'll read it to her.

He reads aloud. 'Anthony and Wendy Hark have been officially listed as people of interest in the disappearance of Jason and Holly Holloway . . .' He scrolls down further, pleased to see that they apparently went missing at the corner of Wallen and Masterton two nights ago, which means their scene worked.

She's puzzled by the phrase 'people of interest' and asks him what it means.

'It's a good thing,' he says. He pockets the phone. His hand hurts. His vision is blurry around the edges. 'It means we're almost finished.'

She tells him to give her back the phone.

'She's tricked you, you idiot. Once you turn it on, they can track it. We can't use it anymore.' He says this with his usual confidence, the way he regularly lies to her to get what he wants, playing on both her adoration for him and her general stupidity. He doesn't know whether they can track phones any more than he knows whether they can listen through the walls. That's not the point. A week ago he could have told her the front lawn was boiling lava and not to go outside, and she would have believed him and obeyed. But he can tell that she doesn't believe him anymore. His control is slipping.

But that's okay, he reasons. They are almost done. Though he's not entirely sure he believes that himself anymore. Nevertheless, he chants it to himself like a mantra. They are almost done. *People of interest* is good. Not long to go.

CHAPTER 25

Claudette

It's a two-hour drive to the South City Centre for Youth Rehab-
ilitation. The front entrance, replete with barbed wire, is as
charming as the name. The mayor decided a few years ago that he
didn't like the phrase 'Juvenile Detention Centre', but the rebrand
doesn't make it feel any more welcoming. The gates swing open as
they approach.

On the drive, Claudette put a call in to Graham Mullins and
asked him to throw his FBI weight around. He's made sure the
Centre will be expecting her and said he'd put out an alert to all
agencies, just in case the Harks had left the state, and even promised
he could have an agent to her by tomorrow to assist Connell's investigation. 'Fuck it,' he said, near the end of the call. 'Let's leak it to
the press. Smoke them out.'

'We're basing this on a hunch and some parking tickets. Is that
legal?'

'If I say it's legal, it's legal.' Mullins assured her he'd say they
were 'people of interest' and that way, if they came forward and
were innocent, they couldn't sue.

Claudette could tell Davies was thinking she was doing *spy shit*.

He had his own task for the drive, keeping in touch with Connell, who had sent officers to the Harks' home. 'Sorry, Claude,' he said about ten miles out. 'Empty.'

As they park, she asks Davies to stay in the car. 'Callum is going to be'—she isn't sure how to explain it to him—'surprised to see me. Seeing a uniformed cop as well isn't going to help.'

He agrees, saying he needs to call Connell with an update anyway. She can tell that he's a little disappointed, even though he's brushing it off.

The reception attendant, wearing a grey shirt made of material so cheap it would be a challenge to find someone *not* allergic to it, has a creeping rash up his neck. He scans her in, takes her phone and two ballpoint pens from her pocket, and gives her a visitor's ID on a lanyard. He makes a phone call, sliding glances back towards her. Eventually he hangs up.

'Doesn't want to see you.' He shrugs. Before she can protest, he says, 'I know you're FBI or whatever, that's fine. But I can only put you in a room with him if he agrees. It's my arse.'

'Ask him again.'

'Lady, I'm sorry. We offered him food, a hot chocolate. Normally they go for that, but the kid says he's never met, and doesn't want to speak to, Claudette Holloway.'

'In that case, tell him Raphael Lopez is here.'

Callum is a freckled, curly-haired boy with shoulders that have gone through puberty ahead of the rest of him, giving him the appearance of a bobble-headed car ornament. He's wearing a bright yellow jumpsuit. That was another rebranding idea from the mayor, who thought orange made inmates feel like prisoners, and yellow would be more 'joyous'. A guard ushers him in, then closes the door and stands outside. The facility is medium security, so he's not shackled.

Claudette doesn't think he looks intimidating, especially compared to some of the boys who wind up in here, but then she remembers he plotted to torture his science teacher, and changes her mind.

'You grew tits, Raph,' he says, sitting down on the flimsy aluminium chair set out for him.

'Kids these days grow up so fast,' she says.

'I *knew* something was up. I still can't believe I fell for it. You didn't even sound like a real teenager. I just thought you were, you know, Spanish or some shit. When those SWAT guys kicked down my parents' door – I knew it was 'cause of Raphael. I thought you were some fat cop behind a desk, though. I can't believe it's *you*.'

There's something is his tone that unnerves her, particularly on the word *you*. She puts it down to his leering sexism, that he can't believe a woman outsmarted him.

'Are you here to gloat?'

'Callum, I put you here to protect others at your school. But I also put you here to protect you. You might not appreciate it now, but I stopped you from ruining your life.'

'I was just going to scare him,' Callum says, sulking. 'It was only a stun gun. It's not like I was going to shoot up the school. People in here are way worse than I am.' He looks up at her and there are tears in his eyes.

She thinks for a second about what's at stake if she gets it wrong. If she points the finger at some harmless kid who's just pumped up on bravado without any real intent. The FBI's powers to combat terror threats are unprecedented, its pre-emptive authority to detain a suspect almost limitless, regardless of whether the suspect would have followed through on their threats. Of course, if such aggressive preventive measures work, then there's no attack to prove the suspect was dangerous, so paradoxically, they can seem unnecessary and overbearing. But when it doesn't work – when a black van and stretchers are lined up outside a *primary school*, when a coffin-maker gets twice as much work for the same amount of wood – it's the opposite: everyone sees the failure. The trick is to know how hard to push, where to set the boundary. Was Callum what happens on the edge of that boundary? He's blubbering now.

'You have to take me out early. I don't fit in here. You're here to help me, right?'

She's reminded so much of Jason, she almost reaches out and hugs him, but holds back.

When he sees the waterworks aren't working, Callum huffs. 'You're a fucking bitch, you know that? You spend all your time following boys on the internet? I can think of another word for that.'

She decides the line is in the right place. 'Your parents may have done something terrible,' she says. 'I need to ask you about them.'

'If I answer your questions, will you help my parole?'

'It can't hurt.'

'So, no, then.' He rocks back on two legs of the chair, pushing his tongue inside his cheek.

'No.' She drums her fingers on the table. 'But you're going to help me, because you'll get out of here sometime in the not-too-distant future, and you're going to have to either visit your parents some-where similar or bring flowers to their graves. I don't know what will happen if a SWAT team gets to them before I do. Your choice.'

Callum doesn't say anything. Claudette is well versed in teenage-speak and knows that means he's agreed to go along with it.

'How did your parents react to you being accused?' she asks.

'How do you think?' Callum says. 'Mum was just crying all the time: she had to stop watching the news, she lost her appetite, she stopped going to work, let the agency just grind to a halt. She couldn't concentrate on anything. She could barely string a sentence together without bursting into tears, and eventually she stopped trying altogether. It felt like, you know, every day there was a little bit less of her. She just got real quiet.'

'And your father?'

'He kind of lost it. Took it out on me. He took it out on her, too. Like, didn't hit her or nothing that I saw, but it was all he could do to stop himself.'

'You'd say he was mad?'

'All the time. Look, let me put it this way, I was on bail at home for most of the trial. By the time they carted me off here, I was glad to go. Because home wasn't home anymore.'

Claudette feels heat prickling at the back of her neck. That was another problem inherent in her job. Instead of stopping one monster, had she created a different one?

'Is there somewhere they might go? To hide out?'

'Hide out? My parents?' He laughs. 'My folks aren't *fugitives*.'

'If they were, where might they go?'

'Ah . . .' He can't think of an answer. 'I really don't know. They don't have some secret cabin in the woods, if that's what you mean.'

'Your parents know who I am. I know Raphael's messages were used in the pre-trial, while we were still looking at adult charges, but the FBI makes sure I never testify in public.' The judge had been worded up in private, to make sure it wasn't entrapment, but once they got to the public trial and the charges were downgraded and the FBI removed, with Callum entering into a plea bargain, the messages didn't need to be admitted. 'There's no way anything could have leaked from the trial. So how have they figured it out? What did you tell them about me? About Raphael?'

'Nothing. I assumed you were a fake but I didn't know it was you until you walked in the door just now. Makes sense, though. Jason thinks you're a prostitute,' Callum says. 'No offence. I'm just saying.'

Her son's name, from this boy's lips, stuns her. She rethinks her unease at one of the first things he said to her – '*I can't believe it's you.*' – and understands his tone better now. He knows her. 'Jason?'

'Yeah, you're his mum, right? Weird that you stay home all day. That's what all his friends say, that it's so you can take *appointments*. He plays along.'

His smile is lecherous, but she's not paying attention. It's all crashing together. That was how the Harks could have figured out who she was, they followed her son. How long had they planned this? Watched her? Watched him?

'You can't have been friends, I would have known,' she pleads.

Jason didn't mix with the Callums of the world. She knew that. Then she remembers Lucas's mother telling her 'They're not really friends anymore.' She remembers the feeling of no longer recognising any of his friends as she scrolled his friends list. *Lucas says Jason's not exactly one of the more popular kids.* She realises, when she was logged in as Raphael, that she and Jason had exactly one mutual friend.

Despite everything making sense, she manages a futile stammer. 'You're . . . lying.'

'You don't know the half of it.'

'What do you mean?'

'They played that video in court, more times than I can count.' Callum is smiling now. Claudette knows what he means by that video. She remembers Callum being centre frame, jabbing at the squirrel with the stun gun. The camera shaking with laughter, held by a second person he'd never given up during the trial. She wills him not to say it, but he does: 'Who do you think held the camera?'

Claudette is fuming as she leaves the centre, striding across the car park in the now-dark, clenching and unclenching her fists. She should be mad at Jason. If she could be sure he was safe she'd be furious with him. But instead she's pummelling herself. She thought she was doing well on her own. She prided herself on protecting her children. But now all of that, how she defines herself as a human being, as a mother, is crumbling. She isn't the only one in the family wearing a mask. She spent so long looking for flaws in other people's children, she never saw them in her own.

Her blindness to so much of Jason's development (the evil voice inside tells her it's because he doesn't have a father – she tells it to fuck off) had let him mix with the wrong crowd, and it had put him and Holly right in the path of two psychopaths. Psychopaths she had created.

She can tell, as she opens the car door, that Davies is trying to read in her expression what she's learned inside. Even without a mirror, she knows what's etched across her features: her new mask. It's the same look of discovery she saw earlier on the woman in the waiting room of the police station. *So, this is my son.*

She doesn't know how yet, but if the Harks figured out that Claudette was involved in convicting Callum, they'd be angry, sure, but when they also found out that *her* son had got away with the same crime, they'd be murderous. They wouldn't trust the police or the FBI after that; they'd see the whole system as corrupt. They'd realise they had no choice but to take matters into their own hands. Their motive was revenge, but it was also a warped sense of justice.

The Harks will never call; she knows this now. They want to punish her. If she doesn't find her children soon, she'll have to bury them.

CHAPTER 26

Him

His arm doesn't feel like it belongs to him anymore. Everything below the elbow feels numbed, like when you sit on your hand. The pain has set up camp, a constant throb that is setting him on edge. He's convinced it's the Boy's fault. Even though he cut himself to write the words with his own blood on the footpath, somehow he feels the Boy is responsible. He did something to the scissors. He must've. Luna's plan was perfect.

He needs sleep but he doesn't want to let Celeste out of his sight. He keeps his uninjured hand in his pocket, the cool metal of the basement and handcuff keys calming him somewhat, reminding him he's in control. He mustn't let Celeste back down there with them: they are planning something against him. But he can't let them know he knows. Let them think they're planning in secret, he thinks, and they'll fall right into your hands. And as long as he has the keys, Celeste can't do anything.

And if any of them are stupid enough to try, Callum would be proud to know his stun gun will be put to proper use.

Not long to go, he thinks. It's Day Three, and Day Three is *special*. He's been thinking that all day, but only now does it click in his brain why. It really *is* special. She doesn't deserve it, he thinks, but then he figures it's best to keep her close, even though he can't trust her. He still needs her at the end.

Her finds her lying in the front room, curled into a ball on the soft carpet. She hasn't spoken to him since he took the phone away. In fact, she's barely moved. He knows it's because she wants to lie down, but upstairs smells like vomit, so she's chosen the most comfortable spot down here. But one time he walked past and thought she was talking through the floor. The basement's not even under this room, but still, he swore he saw her talking. Maybe through the pipes.

He sits down beside her. 'What are they saying?'

She rolls onto her back, looking at him like he's lost it. Still doesn't speak.

'Truce?' he says, trying to give her his warmest smile. It feels like he's just baring his teeth, but it's the best he can do. 'It's Day Three. You thought I'd forget.'

She tells him he did forget, pouting, then rolls back over.

'Nuh-uh. I saved this for you.' He puts on the voice he uses to talk down to her. He still has the chocolate bar from the supermarket. He's kept it hidden from her to eat himself, but he figures this is a good use for it. He places it on the carpet, right in her eyeline.

She sits up, teary, and wipes a long line of snot up her forearm. She looks at the chocolate and he can tell she wants it. She has no self-control. Just basic human functions. To think he was worried that *she* would ever get the upper hand.

She can't believe he remembered. She picks up the treat. And he has her.

'Of course, I remembered, silly! Especially a big birthday like this one! Ten is *suuuuch* a big number. Double digits!' He ruffles her hair. 'Almost all grown up.'

DAY FOUR

CHAPTER 27

Holly

I think my brother is losing his mind.

He said this would be easy. He said he had a perfect plan. And at the start it *had* seemed perfect. It had felt dangerous and fun. I was on this crazy adventure with my older brother. That was extra nice because I'd struggled to get even half a smile out of him recently. But then he'd invited me on this adventure. He'd said he needed *my* help. I felt as tall as a building.

I had to leave my bag behind first. We spread out all my stuff. Jason said he'd come back and get it after we were done because I like my bag, but he still hasn't gone. Jason also said that if we did it near the place where the cars always crash it would look better. He said it was like making a set for a movie. I'd been deciding whether my bag looked better standing up or knocked over, when I heard Jason yelp and say one of those f-words he isn't supposed to use. He was holding my scissors and blood was dripping between his knuckles. I tried to help him, but he said he was fine and that we had to hurry up.

Mr and Mrs Hark had been where Jason said they would be, because he knew Mrs Hark drives her husband home from his job at the retirement place. My job was to run up to them, as worried and scared as possible. I had to be careful not to be seen by the mean old man at Calm Springs. I try to avoid him anyway. I'd use one of Jason's f-words to describe that mean old man. Jason told me to put on my best acting and I did. I knew it was good because as soon as I told Mr and Mrs Hark my friend was playing around in the house across the road and had hurt themselves, I could barely keep up with them running. Jason had already broken the lock when he dropped off our supplies during his free period, and he'd hidden in the house to surprise them, while I made sure the door was closed and kept watch. Jason got that thing he calls a zapper and the hand-cuffs from his friend Callum, who isn't around after school anymore but Jason never told me why. The zapper did what he said it would on Mr Hark – put him straight to sleep. I tried not to look during that bit. Jason told me it wouldn't hurt, though, like how he padded the cuffs so they wouldn't hurt their wrists. Mrs Hark didn't go to sleep but she did everything Jason told her to.

Once we were in the house is when everything started to go bad. I wasn't allowed to use his name anymore – we had to call each other something different. And we had to call the Harks the Girl and the Boy, just in case people were listening. But he let me choose the codenames. I chose Princess Luna and Princess Celestia from my favourite TV show: *My Little Pony*. He told me to grow up, which wasn't very nice, but he liked it when I suggested we cut the Princess bit and make Celestia easier to pronounce. He ruffled my hair that way he does and said what a great team we made.

The codenames were just the first of his rules. I wasn't allowed near the basement – that was another one. He said he'd carry them down the stairs, and I tried to ignore the noises coming from the basement while I watched the front yard. There were thuds and yelling, and eventually I had to look. I wasn't expecting Mr Hark to be still asleep at the bottom of the stairs. He was lying down, and there was something on his face. I couldn't tell if it was blood or not. Then Mrs Hark saw me, and I knew Jason would be so mad, so I ran back to the kitchen and waited for him there.

He'd promised we wouldn't hurt them. That was the first promise he broke, even though I don't think I really knew he'd broken it until later. He'd promised me lots of things, like that it would be over quickly. He'd promised Mrs Hark was weak. That was a lie. Sometimes I thought he was even scared of her.

It was more fun planning it – sitting in his room talking about our codenames, him teaching me cool things like the word *accomplice* – than it was actually doing it. We didn't have enough stuff, because we'd only taken whatever Mum wouldn't notice was gone. Though I knew she'd – as Jason would say – 'go apeshit' if she couldn't find the kitchen torch. And she hates her tea black, but we took the milk anyway.

But ever since that first night he's just got more and more mad. He's been stomping around nursing his sore hand, which has puffed up like a balloon, and he keeps poking and pushing it like I did when my tooth wouldn't fall out. I really thought he was going to kill Mr Hark when he said Jason was *acting like an f-word-ing child*. I think Jason quite liked pretending to be a grown-up and having them do what he wanted, and that's why he got mad. But I could tell Mr and Mrs Hark were upset. That's why I chose my very favourite chocolate cereal for them, because I thought they needed a special treat and I always like Chocolate Cheerios when I'm feeling sad. Wow, though, he really made a scene when that old lady tried to help me at the supermarket. She was just offering to call my mummy, because I'd put a few lollies in my pocket. I thought he'd forgiven me because I used the f-word at her. But then Jason got drunk, like Mummy does sometimes, and he'd tried to touch Mrs Hark the way teenage boys want to touch girls, but I knew that wasn't allowed. And then I don't know how I made him mad too, but I did. That's when he locked me in the basement.

While I was sitting in the dark thinking I must deserve it, Mrs Hark started to whisper to me. She'd told me before that he was dangerous, but I think I started to believe her then, even if it took me a little longer to figure it out properly. Now I'm sure. I told her it was okay. I told her we had a plan and everything would work out all right. Sometimes adults just don't shut up, though. She kept whispering at me most of the night. She told me some things she said I didn't have to tell Jason. It was nice to have secrets of my own.

But Jason told me she would do this. That the Harks would try to convince me to talk to them. That's why he didn't want me in the basement in the first place, he said. Aside from the hurting (though he told me the Harks were bad people and no one would miss them anyway), everything else was still going the way he said it would. He said that once we made the news, we only needed one more night before we let them go. That was what I was looking forward to. Because when we do go home, we're going to say that *we* escaped from *them*. It will be our word against theirs, he said. And, even better, we'll be *famous*. That stupid TV guy in his suit and gelled hair telling me I was 'too boring for us, honey'. He'll have to shut up. Jason said this will make me really famous, like in other countries too, all over the world. I'll be a hero. I know I'm never going to make it on those stupid road trips to Vegas, where all Mum wants to do is eat pizza and wear bathrobes in hotel rooms. She doesn't seem to realise how important these opportunities are. But if we're the kids who were not only abducted, but who *escaped*, people will want to talk to me – that's what Jason says. All the judges will hit their buzzers. He said they'll even make a movie out of it. I could star as myself!

That's why it was important to choose a spot where it looked like a car picked us up. That's why he had to write the message in blood, and why he didn't bring much food to eat, because it has to look like we haven't eaten much when we get out. He said it's all a *story* – what we can make it look like. That's why he invited me along: a teenage boy is not interesting enough, but I have the 'cute factor'. 'Clickbait' is the word he used.

I'd asked him, before this, why he wanted to do this. I didn't think he liked singing and acting and stuff like I did. I thought he just liked shooting people on his video games.

'These people might know something about me that I would rather they didn't,' he said. I told him I didn't get it, and what did that have to do with getting famous anyway?

'Well, Celeste,' he said, winking at me, and I'd giggled because I still liked being called Celeste back then, 'you want to be famous, and I want to be infamous.'

I didn't understand what he meant at the time. I still don't know what the word means. But I think, now that I'm here, that maybe he just wants to hurt someone. I try to picture how he feels. How it felt when he made me use the zapper on Mrs Hark. She'd screamed like it hurt more than Jason said it would . . . My heart was beating really quickly after that. I felt sick and dizzy too.

But I know it will be worth it. Once we let them go, it will all be behind me and I'll just smile for the cameras and hang out with celebrities. No one ever made it big without putting in a bit of hard work. That's another word Jason taught me: *sacrifice*.

I'm eating the chocolate bar he left me, and I think he thinks that I've forgiven him. The carpet is scratchy on the back of my neck. He's changing all the time, and he's starting to look at me funny, like he knows I'm up to something. Like when Mum knows I've made a mess or broken something and I'm trying to hide it from her. Just before, when I was trying out a quick prayer, just to see if it worked, because that's what people in movies do, he thought I was talking through the floor. I need to be more careful.

I like that, because of Mrs Hark whispering to me through the night, I have some secrets he doesn't know. That makes me feel good. She told me a lot of interesting things. *Just between us*, she said, quiet and giggly, like when my friend Mel is allowed to sleep over. For starters, she told me Mr Hark's phone password. Even though I can't read all the big words properly and Jason had to read the news for me, that was my secret to share. Jason would be so mad if he knew what else Mrs Hark had told me. He'd use the f-word. A whole bunch. She told me so many secrets.

She told me that she'll make sure I don't get in trouble if I help her get out.

She told me the real word for the zapper thing he keeps waving around: *stun gun*. And she told me Jason left his empty wine bottle down there with her.

CHAPTER 28

Claudette

Davies has the siren on, flooring it. Claudette spent the first hour of their drive on a conference call with Connell and Mullins, both pulled away from their washing-up duties or late-night whiskeys. Thankfully they didn't indulge in any haggling over jurisdiction and the two quickly agreed to work together (though she wished she could have seen Connell's face when Mullins referred to her as an FBI '*asset*'). There is now a national alert for the Harks, in case they flee the state, and Connell has a unit over at their residence. The last he heard it was clean, but they were about to 'fuck the place up'. Davies has done his best to stay out of it, keeping his eyes on the road, white knuckles on the wheel, as he decides how much he can push the engine and how much he's allowed to eavesdrop on an FBI conversation. It's just gone midnight and they're crossing the edge of town when Mullins signs off with, 'Don't worry, we're bringing the cavalry.'

'So Callum and your son were friends?' Davies asks, finally getting a word in.

'Apparently,' she replies. 'I didn't know. Some detective, to miss that.'

'None of this is your fault.'

'It's my job to know my son.'

'Let me ask you this then. These kids you find online, the ones who are planning all kinds of horrors – when their parents are in court, on the news, do they look like they knew? Did the Harks?'

She realises she's bone tired, rubs at her forehead. 'I tried, you know. I took him to football practice. I know what video games he likes. He's never playing one of those again once I get him back, that's for sure. I tried my best, but I only scratched the surface. And it's going to get both him and Holly killed.'

She doesn't want Davies to see her cry, but the tears start anyway. He shifts uncomfortably in his seat.

'I'm trying to hate them, I really am. But I can't, not fully, because I *am* them. I am the Harks. I am the mother of a boy who hurts animals.'

'I'm not a parent,' Davies says, 'so take this with a grain of salt, but no one knows their kids. My parents didn't know shit about me. It's how you respond that makes you different to them, Claude.'

She finds herself reaching out for his hand. He lets her take it.

'Past midnight,' he says, glancing down at the dash. She knows what he means. *Day Four.*

Four days, three nights: for children who've been abducted it's usually too late. In a strange way, Claudette feels less anxious about the time now, because she figures the Harks must have something planned, and whether it's day one or day four or day twenty-five, there's still a plan.

'They're still alive, they have to be,' she says. 'The terror suspects I track, any school shooter, it's about fame . . . well, infamy. This has to be the same thing. Except they're not doing it to get on the news, it's not for the history books, it's not even for God. It's for me.'

'*Find us.*' Davies recites the bloodied words. 'They definitely want you to come for them.'

'So, day four. What would you do?' she asks.

He thinks for a second, then decides on an answer but doesn't want to say it. She can tell because his hand clenches hers much tighter.

'You can say it,' she says.

'I'd kill one of them.' He doesn't look at her.

He's right. Holly was probably taken because one pound of flesh isn't enough; they want two. They want to hit Claudette twice as hard as she hit them, and fuck karma. But a second victim has a second purpose. It gives them the opportunity to send her a message.

'If they did it already,' Davies continues, 'the body would be easy to find because they'd want you to see it.' He's trying to make her feel better, but it isn't really working. He changes the topic. 'What if they run?'

'Mullins has security notified at the airports, but that won't matter, because they can't leave the country. The kids don't have passports.'

She can tell Davies wants to tell her that the Harks *could* very well leave the country if they leave the kids behind, but he lets it go. He knows she needs to believe they're alive.

'If they're not done with you, they'll want to stay close,' he indulges her.

She doesn't say anything, turning everything over in her mind, when suddenly the car lurches and she's violently jolted in her seat. Her forehead bounces off the side window, and the seatbelt pulls tight enough across her chest to bruise.

'Fucking idiot!' Davies yells, leaning on the horn. A bus has just cut them off, forcing Davies to swerve into another lane. 'My lights are on and everything,' he says with a *tsk*. He looks over at her, his brow creased in concern. 'Are you okay? Did you hit your head? You look pale. Jesus, Claude, you're scaring me. Say something.'

Claudette is not concussed, she's just stunned by what she's seen: Wendy Hark, staring out at her, plastered to the back of the bus.

Callum had mentioned her working at *the agency* but it hadn't clicked yet. Wendy Hark is a realtor. Which means she has a portfolio of houses for sale: empty properties.

If they get a list, Mullins or Connell can search them all in a few hours. But they won't have to. Claudette can already see the sign in her mind. Right across the road from Calm Springs. Walking distance. The garden unkempt, the shrubbery blocking out the middle of the words so it just reads *Hate*. Remove the bushes and it's the logo on the bus that almost pancaked them thirty seconds ago: *Hark's Real Estate*.

She thinks the revelation deserves a victorious whoop, but her mouth has gone so dry it barely rasps out. 'I know where they are.'

CHAPTER 29

Holly

'We're done,' Jason says. 'It's enough.'

I haven't slept, and neither has he. Neither of us wants to take our eyes off the other one, so we're sitting on opposite sides of the lounge seeing who'll doze off first. It has a name – a Mexican thing. We're doing that.

I'm pretty sure I'll win. I'm tired, but I had chocolate. Jason looks like he might fall asleep any minute. He actually looks like he might fall down dead, if I'm honest. Even sitting down he's swaying on the spot, cradling his sore hand in his lap. His face has gone a pasty white, which makes his lips look bright red. I think he's really starting to lose it. He told me to stop talking through the floor again a little while ago, even though this time I wasn't even praying.

'It's over?' I say, not sure if he's trying to trick me. 'We're going home?'

He shuts his eyes and mumbles. 'We're going home.' He sounds exhausted.

'Can I tell them?'

He grunts back.

I stand up and walk over, poke him in the shoulder. 'Can I tell them?'

He opens his eyes and looks up at me. His forehead is crinkled. He's confused. Like *I'm* the one not making sense. 'Why?'

'I just want to,' I say. I don't say that I want to tell Mrs Hark especially, but it's true. She'll be so happy.

He shrugs, then hauls himself up the way Dad used to pull himself out of the La-Z-Boy after too many beers. I hold out my hand for the keys, but he shakes his head. He silently walks over to the basement door and holds himself up against the frame. He misses the keyhole three times, but eventually he gets the key in. He hands me the torch. 'Be quick,' he grunts.

I bound down the stairs. Mr Hark is lying on his side, curled up against the wall, asleep, and I don't want to wake him yet, so I cross the room to Mrs Hark. Her eyes go tiny in my bouncing light. She gives me a tired smile.

'Guess what?' I say.

'You're in a good mood.' Her voice is scratchy, and I try to remember if we gave them more water. We probably should have. It doesn't matter now.

'We're letting you go,' I say and wait for her face to explode with joy. If she wasn't chained up – and we'll fix that nice and quick – she'd probably jump up and down too.

I'm confused when she doesn't say anything. She just bows her head and shakes it. Her dark, greasy hair hangs in knotted clumps on her shoulders. 'Did he give you the key?' she whispers, and when I don't say anything she adds, 'He's not going to let us go.'

'He is. He just told me. We're in the news. We did three nights, that's good enough. Now we just go home.'

'None of us can just go home after this.' She raises her head and her teeth are all squeezed together like an angry dog. She thrusts her chin across the room. 'Tony is practically unconscious. He needs medical help. His injuries will speak for themselves. I know your brother padded the cuffs so it wouldn't look like we were chained up, but he was too hot-headed to leave us uninjured. There's too much evidence here. Everyone will know it was you.'

'No.' I realise she just doesn't understand. I'm so silly: once I explain it to her it will be fine. 'We say that you guys did it. Then there's a movie and stuff. You can come with me to LA. We'll go to the premiere.'

'Jesus.' She says this under her breath but I hear it. Why isn't she happy about this? 'You've really got no fucking clue, do you?'

'What did you just—'

'Hurry up!' Jason calls from the top of the stairs. 'Bring the bucket with you.'

'He's going to kill us,' Mrs Hark says. She's talking quickly now. 'If we're alive, we can tell the police what happened here, and don't think I don't recognise that stun gun he's been using. Callum might not have turned him in, but he'll be scared as shit that we will. We spent a fortune on that lawyer, and Callum was still lucky to get two years. Jason's older than him; he won't be so lucky. And if the charges are federal, that's ten years in an adult prison. He gets off on hitting us while we're tied up. He's a coward. He'd probably do this no matter how long they'd lock him up for. He's scared of being pinned as an accomplice.'

I recognise the word 'accomplice', because Jason taught it to me, but other than that I have no idea what she's talking about. She's gone crazy down here in the dark for too long.

'It's not some stupid game, like you seem to think it is. Killing us is the only way out of it. Plus, I think he just wants to. I see the same thing in him I saw in my son, once I knew who he really was. It's never been about letting us go. It took me a while to figure out why you're here, but he's tricked you too.'

I almost laugh. 'He's not going to *kill* you.'

'Where did you get the cereal, the bottles of water? There are security cameras at every supermarket. Someone will have seen you, and then they'll know you left this house *on your own* when you were supposed to be tied up in the basement. The only way they don't dig further is if you tie up all the loose ends right here and now and it all goes down quickly enough that no one thinks to ask questions or take a second look. He's not as clever as he thinks he is – we've got injuries, the toilet bucket has our DNA in it . . . There are clues to prove that we're down here and you're up there. But when the alternative is something so *unbelievable* . . . it might just work. And that's why he's going to kill us.'

None of what she's saying makes any sense. We're kids, he's always said it, so everyone will believe us. That was why I was here: the cute factor. Everyone will believe me, just like Mr and Mrs Hark did when I ran up to them, lip quivering, and begged for them to help me. I wonder if she's lying about cameras at the supermarket. Jason said people could listen through walls and I'm not sure I believe him, but Mrs Hark sounds serious.

'Listen,' she whispers. She shuffles up to her knees to get closer. Her elbows are bent, with her hands held up by the pipe. It looks like she's at church. Or asking for money. Begging: that's the word. 'It's not too late for you to fix this. You haven't done much, legally speaking. You're too young anyway. I'll tell them he had you under duress. It's not too late. But once he comes down here, it will be.'

'What do you mean?'

'If you help me, I'll help you.'

'I am helping you,' I say slowly.

'You're not . . .' She realises she's raised her voice and gives me another smile. But it looks more like Jason's now. Like she's glued it on. 'You're not listening. You need to help us. He will not let us go. You need to get the keys from him.'

I shake my head. 'He's in charge of the keys. That's one of the rules.'

'Oh, God.' She slumps back to the floor, leaning her head against the wall. 'My life is in the hands of a child.'

'I am not a child.' I puff my chest up. 'I'm very grown-up, actually. And I wouldn't lie to you. You're my friend.'

Then she gives me the meanest look I've ever got in my entire life. 'You are not my friend. You don't even know what you've done,' she growls. 'Leave me alone to die in peace, little girl.'

CHAPTER 30

Claudette

If the stop sign on the corner of Masterton and Wallen hadn't already been knocked over, Davies would have done it himself. He swings the car too sharply around the corner and mounts the kerb. He wrenches the wheel and slams on the brakes with a loud squeal, and they barely miss what's left of the sign.

Claudette raises a finger to her lips. Davies flicks the headlights off and crawls up to the house. They radioed ahead for every available officer, but they have still arrived first. She doesn't know how far away the back-up is – they've asked them to approach without sirens in case the Harks have itchy trigger fingers – but for the moment, they seem to be on their own.

The house is modest, two storeys and painted white, with triangular awnings and gutters like a gingerbread house. There are big windows that look out onto the street. The curtains are drawn. Claudette wonders if she's already been spotted: going into Calm Springs, talking with Davies in his patrol car earlier this afternoon. She feels a knot in her stomach. What if that is what they wanted? What if her getting close is the cue for their next move? But she can't think about 'what ifs' anymore. Now is the time to act.

Claudette starts to get out of the car, but Davies grabs her arm before she can open the door.

'Tactical will be here in less than five minutes,' he says, shaking his head. 'We can't go in without them.'

'They might not have five minutes, Will.'

'It could endanger them if we go in early.'

'Please.'

'We can't. We have orders.'

'*You* have orders. I'm a civilian, remember?'

He lets go of her but doesn't move. 'You're unarmed.'

She thinks for a second. 'Give me your gun.'

'What?'

'Your gun, give it to me. You can say that I took it. By force.'

'You're joking. Even if you don't shoot anybody—'

'I will spend the rest of my life in prison to keep my children safe.' She holds out her hand.

Davies puts his hands in a cone over his mouth and swears. Then he sighs, unclasps his holster and hands her the gun. 'I'll say you stole it. I'm not hitting myself in the face like in the movies, though.'

CHAPTER 31

Holly

'She says you're going to kill them,' I say, when I reach the top of the stairs, putting the toilet bucket down.

He is still stooped against the frame. His shoulders twitch like he's silently laughing, but he doesn't answer me. He wrenches himself upright, wobbles and goes to walk past me, down to them.

'Hey!' I punch him in the back of the shoulder. 'It's not true!' I am shaking my head so I believe it. 'It's not true.'

He turns, stretches his back and all of a sudden he's towering over me. His words are slurred, like he's talking in slow motion. Like when he drank the wine. 'What did you think was going to happen?'

'You can't kill them!' I'm yelling now. There is a squeal some-where up the street, like the sound a car makes when smoke comes out of its wheels. I go for the door. 'This wasn't the plan.'

His hand grabs my shoulder and squeezes hard enough to hurt. He shoves me back from the door so hard I bump into the oppo-site wall.

'Think about it, for fuck's sake, Holly!' He must be mad; he's used my real name. 'This is all about what it *looks like*. We're saying

we escaped. We're saying these'—he points down the stairs—
'*animals* kept us prisoner for four days. We've used weapons and
handcuffs that only they could have gotten, left over from their son.
We've used a house they have access to. When we do it, I can make
it look like we fought back. We can even hurt each other a little bit if
we need to. I can disguise their injuries as us fighting back. The cuffs
won't have left marks on their wrists. Everything the police will have
seen so far, and when they find us covered in blood, running down
that street, screaming for help, points to the Harks. But when we
leave this place, there are two people left who can put their hands
up and say that none of that is true, that what we're saying didn't
happen. They'll turn on us. Not only because of what we've done
here, but also what I did with . . . well, that doesn't matter.'

I wonder if he's talking about the same thing Mrs Hark was,
down in the basement. Something about his friend Callum.

'And if the cops listen to them and start looking at things
properly, they're bound to find something that shows we're lying.
That means it needs to be a slam dunk. No one can ask questions.
No one.'

He picks up the toilet bucket and walks away from me. I hear
the back door open. He's gone maybe twenty seconds, and then he
comes back without the bucket. He's getting rid of clues, I realise.

'The cameras in the supermarket?' I stutter, figuring it out.

'What? Yeah. Sure.' That catches him off guard, and his head
does a little shake. I worry I've given away one of Mrs Hark's
secrets. 'Cameras in the stores. I hadn't thought about that. But if
they have no reason to check them, they won't.' He squints, as if
he's just realised something. 'That woman might remember you,
though . . . Shit. We can . . . fix her . . . after. We can fix everything
after. You'll get what you want out of this. All of the attention and
media, and you can be a *survivor*. But it has to be your story. Yours.
Not theirs.' He kneels down to my height and puts on his slightly

deeper, bedtime-story voice that he does when he's trying to make me feel better. 'I'll tell you a secret. That's why you're here. Because if I did this on my own, no one would believe me. But you'—he strokes my cheek—'they'll believe every single thing you say.'

I'm crying now. I can't breathe properly. He stands up, lumbers to the basement doorway, and turns back to me.

'I'm here to kill these people, to see what it feels like. And you're here to help me get away with it.'

I listen to the creak of the stairs as Jason goes down. I hear Mrs Hark start talking, but I can't understand what she's saying. She isn't screaming.

I think about what Mrs Hark said to me. That she'll help me if I help her. That it's not too late to fix things. That word she used: *duress*. I'm not sure what it means but she was talking about the same thing Jason was: who gets believed. She was talking about me and her joining our stories together. Against *him*. She was telling me that maybe that's a better way to get out of this.

I bite my knuckle. I know I can't trust her any more than I can trust Jason. He warned me that she'd play tricks on me if I listened to her. But he's gone crazy. Maybe it's my job now to protect them from him.

I could just go, I suddenly realise. Jason is . . . busy . . . in the basement. The front door lock is smashed. I could just run out the door, run home, and never think about this house or these people ever again.

I find that while I've been thinking about this, I've actually walked over to the door, though I can't remember ever deciding to. I open it a tiny bit, just to see outside. The street is quiet, the grass shiny with evening wetness. I take a breath and get ready to step out.

That's when I see a police car parked across the road, a few houses away. As I'm looking at it, the car door opens. A shadow gets out. It starts coming towards the house.

I shut the door and run for the basement.

CHAPTER 32

Claudette

Claudette hurries across the road, along the footpath and up the path, checking the windows for peering eyes or the glint of a gun barrel. It will do her children no good if she is gunned down on the porch. She's also analysing the yard, planning an exit strategy.

She makes it to the porch without seeing a flutter in the curtains. The front door is ajar. The lock is broken. Why break a lock on a house Wendy Hark has keys for? It seems odd, but she counts it as luck that she can slowly ease open the door without making any noise.

Before she enters the house, she shoots a quick look back to the patrol car. Davies is still in the driver's seat. He's probably doing what he was doing before she left, yelling into the radio for the other cars to hurry up. She knows he won't come after her without back-up, but she's still half expecting to turn and see him jogging up to her from the dark. Not this time. She's on her own.

The truth is, she's thankful Davies hasn't followed her. Because it means that once she gets inside this house, once she is face to face with the monsters who have taken her children, no one else will see what she does to them.

CHAPTER 33

Holly

I don't know exactly what type of horrible thing I am expecting to see in the basement, but what I do see is not it. Jason is standing at the bottom of the stairs, the stun gun ready in his hand. Mr Hark is still asleep, like the last time I came down, flat on his back. Though now I'm not sure he's sleeping. Mrs Hark is sobbing. I've never seen her sob before. She's been so calm and strong through all of this, it's a shock to hear her crying. He's finally broken her, I think. He'll like that. He's won.

'Please,' Mrs Hark is saying. 'He hasn't moved in hours. Just tell me he's still alive.'

Jason looks like he's thinking about it. They both know he's planning to kill them. But maybe it's easier for him to pretend he isn't. He puts his hands up. 'I'll feel his neck,' he says, as nice as I've ever heard him.

Mrs Hark dissolves into blubbering thanks.

Jason goes to where Mr Hark is lying and kneels over him, nodding over to Mrs Hark like he's saying: *I'm doing it. Happy?* Then he puts two fingers under Mr Hark's chin. Mrs Hark can't see it from where she is, but I see Jason slowly slide his thumb around the other side of Mr Hark's neck, until he has his whole hand around it.

And then he starts to squeeze.

Instantly, there is a roar. Mr Hark's body bucks, and Jason is knocked on his side. Mr Hark is moving now. He lands a solid kick to Jason's face as he falls over and then, to my amazement, Mr Hark moves *away* from the wall. The pipe he's chained to is busted where it meets the other pipe, where Mr Hark has spent all that time banging it, not just to annoy Jason with the sound, but to break the whole thing. I can see the screws dangling where it was originally attached to the wall. Mr Hark bends the pipe out of the wall, and then slides his handcuffs along the length until they slip off the end. The pipe sticks out of the wall like a sharp spear.

It's all happening so quickly I haven't even thought about moving. Then there's a loud scream and I realise, weirdly, that it's me.

Jason is on all fours, trying to get up, but Mr Hark's now pulled the wine bottle from his trousers. He smacks it down on the back of Jason's head. It doesn't break; instead there's a *thunk* and Jason's arms and legs all go floppy and he falls on his face. Mr Hark hits him again, and this time the bottle explodes, bits of glass flying everywhere. I pretend it is red wine that splatters the floor.

I've run out of screams. There is now another voice in the room. 'The keys are in his left pocket,' Mrs Hark says.

I realise that Jason hasn't won after all. He hasn't broken her spirit. She's been fake crying. Mr Hark wasn't really unconscious; he'd already broken the pipe and needed Jason to get close. I think how clever she is. Something Jason says comes back to me: *This is all about what it looks like.* They've played him at his own game, made their own little movie set.

Mr Hark has got the keys from Jason's pocket. His handcuffs clink as he drops them. He hurries across to Mrs Hark, but then she lets out a horrible scream. Jason has hauled himself off the ground. I don't see the sharp glass of the broken wine bottle in his hand until he's stabbed Mr Hark in the neck with it. There is no pretending it's wine anymore. I can't believe how much blood comes out. Mr Hark whirls around and it sprays the walls. He drops the handcuff keys. Jason stabs him again. Mr Hark puts his hands to his neck, but blood keeps bubbling out through his fingers and running down his front.

No more acting: now Mrs Hark is crying for real. Mr Hark takes one more half step, but then drops to his knees, gurgles and falls face-forward. He lies still. The pool of red spreads out underneath him.

Jason is wobbling on the spot. Mrs Hark is screaming at him. Jason looks at her. He touches the back of his head with one hand, and it comes away dripping red. He looks at it for a second, like he's surprised. Then he slowly sits down. He leans his back against the wall, and closes his eyes, letting out a long sigh. Then his head drops forward and he doesn't move any more. A long string of red spit hangs from his lips.

Mrs Hark has just seen me on the stairs. 'The keys,' she pleads. 'Please. The keys.'

I turn and run. It's not that I don't want to help her, it's just that there is too much blood. I can't. My brain still can't believe what I've just seen. I head into the corridor, towards the front door. I can hear Mrs Hark's wailing behind me. Only a few steps into the hall, I see the front door start to creep open. What looks like the barrel of a gun pokes its way through.

I don't wait around to see who it is. I am already halfway down the basement stairs again, shutting the door behind me.

CHAPTER 34

Claudette

Claudette uses the barrel of the gun to nudge open the front door. Fragments of voices, like escaping ghosts, flit past her out the door. It sounds like yelling.

She grips the gun tightly, swallowing as she enters. The hallway is empty. The voices are coming from somewhere ahead, but she can't hurry. She's no good to her kids if someone shoots her in the back.

She turns to the right, leading with the gun, looking down the barrel. The front room is lightly furnished, just enough to be appealing to buyers. There's a chocolate wrapper on the floor. She checks the room is clear, then turns back to the corridor. As she moves deeper, there is an acid smell that tickles her throat. Vomit. She shuts her mind to all the bad things that vomit could mean and keeps moving. The kitchen is on her left. There are bottles of water and a blue plastic shopping bag on the counter. She clears the room.

At the base of a flight of stairs, the vomit smell is stronger. It is coming from upstairs. But now she knows where the voices are coming from, a door to her left. They echo like it's a basement.

Some*thing* has happened upstairs, but some*one* is downstairs. Her choice is up or down.

She chooses the basement door. She places one hand on the handle and keeps the gun raised, aimed chest height, with the other, ready to lead with the barrel. She knows she's putting herself in danger. She knows she should wait for back-up. She knows what's behind this door could kill her. But she also knows her children are here. And any concern for her own safety evaporates as her maternal instinct surges. Nothing will stop her.

She opens the door.

CHAPTER 35

Holly

My hands are soaked in blood as I fumble with the handcuff keys, giving them to Mrs Hark. 'It wasn't supposed to go like this,' I say. The tears are splashing down my cheeks. 'Jason . . . I didn't know . . . I'm sorry. I'm so sorry. I'll fix this. I'll fix everything.'

Mrs Hark has one wrist free. 'Listen . . .' She's shaking, seems to keep changing her mind about what to say. 'I just . . . What's already happened has happened. I just want to get out of here.'

'I help you, you help me,' I say.

'Sure,' she replies. The other wrist springs open, and the cuffs clatter to the ground. She examines the keys, like she might need to open some doors, and hangs on to them. She doesn't wait for me, hobbling across the room to check on Mr Hark. She keeps a wary eye on Jason, but we both know he's dead. She rolls Mr Hark over, taps his face, holds his neck and lets out a howl. Then she's up again. She finds the stun gun and picks it up. She seems to remember I'm still here, by the wall, and says to me, 'Stay here. I'll get help.'

Then she runs up the stairs.

I try to do it quietly, but she still hears it when she's halfway up. The soft *click* of a handcuff locking into place.

I see her suddenly figure it all out; it's in the way her face crumples. I've cuffed myself to the wall. She is holding the handcuff keys in one hand, the stun gun in the other, halfway up the stairs. There are two dead bodies on the floor beneath her. Like Jason said, that's all that matters: *what it looks like*. I am no longer crying. She's not the only one who can fake tears. I'm a triple-threat. Plus I have the 'cute factor'. *They'll believe every single thing you say.*

Mrs Hark opens her mouth to say something, but there is a sharp *crack* and her head snaps sideways. A puff of red mist explodes in the air. She wobbles upright for a second or two, then there's another *crack*, and she jerks like she's been punched in the stomach. She tumbles backwards, her whole body floppy, and crashes at the bottom of the stairs.

Mrs Hark told me her secrets, but I didn't tell her mine: I knew somebody was coming into the house. Someone begins to walk down the stairs, so I see bits of them at a time. First I see their legs, then their body, then their outstretched arms, clutching a gun with both hands. Then the rest: it's Mum.

I call out to her, desperate. She sees me, tells me not to move; she needs to make sure it's safe. She checks Mrs Hark's body first, then Mr Hark's. When she checks Jason's, she lets out the same moan Mrs Hark did.

And then she's wrapping me up in her arms, and she's warm and soft and her body is shaking with tears and she holds me so tightly I can hardly breathe. She lets me go so she can kiss my face all over and then touch my cheeks with her fingertips, like she's checking for damage. Then she's squishing me up again in the hug.

'You're safe now,' she says into my hair. 'You're safe now.'

I bury my head in her shoulder and smile.

ACKNOWLEDGEMENTS

While this is only half an acknowledgements section, my full thanks go to:

Karen Yates, Bill Massey and the team at Audible Australia. You took a chance on a then relatively unknown writer and allowed me the freedom and creativity to make bite-sized books with big twists.

Beverley Cousins and the team at Penguin Random House Australia. Thank you for helping me revisit these stories in shiny new print editions. Thank you for indulging my 'can we flip the book upside down' ideas (thanks to Gavin for teaching me it's called a tête-bêche). I am indebted to the genius of Amanda Martin, Phoebe McKenzie, Hannah Ludbrook, Adelaide Jensen, Hannah Armstrong, Janine Nelson, Tanaya Lowden, Sarah McDuling, Anna Ristevski, Gavin Schwarcz, Julie Burland and Holly Toohey for variously pruning, publicising, promoting and sticking with me every step of the way.

Pippa Masson, Caitlan Cooper-Trent and all at Curtis Brown Australia, Kate Cooper and Nadia Farah Mokdad at Curtis Brown UK, and Leslie Conliffe and Kris Karcher at IPG, for all the ingenuity it takes to craft a career.

To the booksellers – thank you for letting me share your shelves, your trust, your customers, and your eyes.

Phew. That was a lot of names and we're only at the interval. Don't worry; like in the theatre, the second half is always shorter.

© Monica Pronk

Benjamin Stevenson is an award-winning stand-up comedian and author. His first novel, *Greenlight*, was shortlisted for the Ned Kelly Award for Best Debut Crime Fiction, and his second novel, *Either Side of Midnight*, was shortlisted for the International Thriller Writers Award for Best Original Paperback.

Everyone In My Family Has Killed Someone, his third novel, was a huge bestseller and has so far been sold in twenty-seven territories around the world. It will soon be adapted into a major HBO TV series. It was shortlisted for the Dymocks Book of the Year 2022, ABIA General Fiction Book of the Year 2023 and BookPeople's Fiction Book of the Year 2023, as well as being named as one of *The Sunday Times*'s best crime novels of 2022. Its sequel, *Everyone On This Train Is A Suspect*, released in October 2023, was another massive international bestseller.

Benjamin has sold out live shows from the Melbourne International Comedy Festival all the way to the Edinburgh Festival Fringe and has appeared on ABC TV, Channel 10 and The Comedy Channel.

Follow Ben to keep up with news,
events and latest releases!

FLIP ME OVER AND START A NEW MYSTERY